Children of Strangers

Children of Strangers

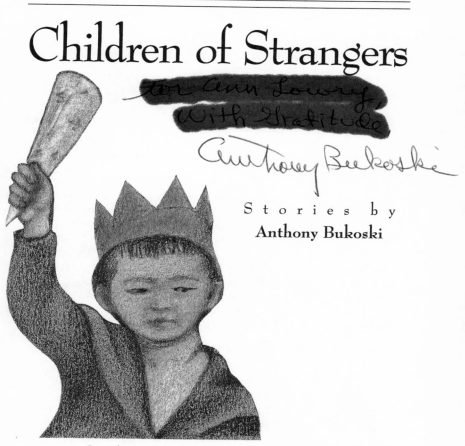

for Ann Lowry,
With Gratitude

Anthony Bukoski

Stories by
Anthony Bukoski

Southern Methodist University Press
DALLAS

These stories are works of fiction. Names, characters, places, and incidents are either the product of the author's imagination or are used fictitiously.

Requests for permission to reproduce material from this work should be sent to:

The stories in this collection first appeared in the following publications: "The Temperature in January" in *Ascent;* "The Perimeter of Light" in *Cimarron Review* (© Board of Regents, Oklahoma State University, reprinted with permission); "Mrs. Burbul" in *Hawai'i Review;* "A Chance of Snow" in *Writer's Forum;* "Country of Lent" in *the minnesota review;* "Old Customs" in *North Dakota Quarterly;* "Children of Strangers" in *Twelve Below Zero* (New Rivers Press); "Tango of the Bearers of the Dead" in *Concert at Chopin's House* (New Rivers Press); "Durum Wheat" in *The Chariton Review;* "Jalousie" in *Quarterly West;* "The Polka-holics" in *Sou'Wester;* "The Tomb of the Wrestlers" (as "Le Tombeau des Lutteurs") in *The Louisville Review;* "The River of the Flowering Banks" in *Beloit Fiction Journal;* and "An Essay on Language" (as "The Fall of Saigon") in *South Dakota Review.*

Library of Congress Cataloging-in-Publication Data

Bukoski, Anthony.
    Children of strangers : stories / by Anthony Bukoski. — 1st ed.
      p.   cm.
    ISBN 0-87074-350-3 (cloth) — ISBN 0-87074-364-3 (paper)
    1. Polish Americans—Superior, Lake, Region—Fiction.
    2. Vietnamese Americans—Superior, Lake, Region—Fiction.
    3. Indians of North America—Superior, Lake, Region—Fiction.
    4. Community life—Superior, Lake, Region—Fiction. I. Title.
    PS3552.U399C45   1993
    813'.54—dc20   93-24483

Design and cover art by Barbara Whitehead

For Elaine

Acknowledgments

I am deeply indebted to Thomas J. Napierkowski, president of the Polish American Historical Association, professor of English, and my friend, for encouraging me in this work; to Michael J. Longrie for his valued criticism; and to the Wisconsin Arts Board and the University of Wisconsin-Superior for their financial support.

Contents

The Temperature

in January

CORPORAL Vankiewicz spent his R&R in a Bang-kok hotel with a pillow over his head. Five floors below were the Bangkok street noises. So he wouldn't hear Wayne Fontana and the Mind-benders' "The Game of Love" or Tom Jones's "What's New, Pussycat?" he avoided bars with jukeboxes, putting cotton in his ears even here in the room.

On the return flight to DaNang, he talked to a Marine who spent his days in tunnels in the wet, rotten earth looking for VC. "Sometimes," the Marine said, "I whisper 'to hell with it' and lay there crying when I hear something. If I panic and claw upwards, I might pop my way between an old man's legs in a grave. Where do you go when you're twelve feet under? Sometimes white roots poke through like fingernails. The roots of what, I don't even know. That's how crazy this war is."

In the C-140 Hercules heading east over the Ruins of Angkor, Vankiewicz had a vision that the country was being undermined by tunnels which would eventually absorb them all. Deep in the Asian earth he would be crawling for his life, crying. Then turning to whoever was grabbing his unbloused boots, he'd sing a popular song:

> Res-cue me,
> from your ten-der charms.
> Res-cue me. . . .

Sometimes in the vision his pursuers would call, "*Anh thường mến* . . ." For several weeks when this thought returned to him—and when the battalion band was done rehearsing for the day—he'd take the cotton out of his ears and cock his head to the ground.

Now, six months later when Vankiewicz had forgotten the tunnel story as he prepared to rotate back to the States, a new battalion drum major joined the band. Vankiewicz saw him when he and Private Borski came back from the dump where each morning old people with teeth black from betel nut waited for the truck to pour creamed beef, eggs, and cornflakes over their heads and arms.

"Isn't it something? Me and the wife," said the new arrival, drum major Longrey, when, of all the wonderful, terrible co-incidences in life, he announced he was from Corporal Vankiewicz's hometown, Superior, Wisconsin. "I was on leave a couple weeks ago, Vankiewicz. Saw it in your records when I got here. We're a couple of home boys."

"I live down by the flour mill, sir."

"You like music, too. Like me, I'll bet," said the drum major who, by rank, was a sergeant major. "You know, I want to make all this ours," he said, pointing with his baton to the horizon. "I want to march from here to Quang Tri, cross the Hai Vans, ford the Song Ben."

In the evenings Vankiewicz walked by the drum major's new tent to see him with an accordion. The other Marines, a year or two removed from high school band concerts, fought with whores in the shanties near the air base or got drunk in DaNang. They did other foolish things—threw "Double E-8" field telephones into the outhouse; drunk, stepped on punji sticks.

Then there was the battalion drum major. Slightly stooped, maybe forty-eight or forty-nine, he had his own failings. He'd play too late into the night or wander beyond the camp's perimeter. Strapping on an accordion and a .45, he would sit alone beyond the compound's listening posts, stare up at Division Ridge, and play "Under the Double Eagle."

He was impressive at the head of the band, though. As he unsnapped the accordion's bellows, pressing its buttons, fingering its keys, he'd say, "Here we go!" and march the men down the red laterite roads, playing "Hello, Dolly," "If Ever I Would Leave You," or "Oklahoma." Old as he is and still at it, thought Corporal Vankiewicz, who was responsible for preparing the get-togethers which occurred every several days in the district hamlets as part of the Pacification Program. After surrounding a hamlet, the infantrymen would round up the inhabitants while ARVN troops searched for VC. By feeding villagers, by entertaining them with a movie in one village, the battalion band in the next, the Americans could win hearts and minds. It was a good deal—"The Star-Spangled Banner," "The Marine's Hymn," then "Bugler's Holiday" or "Semper Fidelis"—marches, show tunes, free food, Tom Jones and Petulah Clark on the loudspeaker.

"How long before you leave for the States, Vankiewicz?" the drum major asked one day when the band returned from An Ho.

"Nineteen short days."

"Not soon enough to suit you, I bet. Why not stay with us, listen to the band. I'll teach you accordion."

"I want to go home, sir."

"But you've got no wife."

"I got friends back home. Before you came one friend, Ed Zimski, was here with Third Shore Party Battalion. He must've rotated by now. I haven't heard much about him. I saw him at the dump a couple months ago," Vankiewicz said, pushing the green utility cap, or cover, back on his head. "Anyway, I hear so much music all the time on Armed Forces Radio and everything that I normally put cotton in my ears. Not now I don't have it in, but normally."

"You're out of uniform you do that," the drum major said. "Take the cotton out for good. You'll never forget it."

The drum major's hair oiled close to his head, his small, wire-rimmed glasses, his pale skin (to keep out of the sun he had a parasol over his director's stand): these gave him the look of a student, Vankiewicz thought. "It's where beauty is in music," the drum major was saying. "I'm telling you, you'll never forget the songs you heard here. 'Don't Sit Under the Apple Tree with Anyone Else but Me'—we had that one in World War II. *'C'est Si Bon'* in Korea. You old enough to remember?" He hummed a little. "Nineteen days? What's so great back home?"

"I don't know. It's sure not the weather or the town. All that broken glass, dust, and paper blowing around."

"I'll bet you can see the radio towers along the Skyline Drive. We may even be neighbors. Ever think of that? Once you're settled, maybe in a month, would you just go for a half-hour, visit my wife? I'll write her, tell her you're going to telephone," the drum major said, adjusting the glasses that appeared to pinch the backs of his ears.

II

Near the end of Vankiewicz's thirteen months, this drum major, who was naturally accorded certain privileges, brought in a housekeeper who had high cheekbones, large, round eyes, and clear skin no cream or powder could improve. When she was with the drum major, she looked as though she'd stepped out of a garden of incense in the morning and, looking up, was surprised to see the company of Marines admiring her. Down her back fell the black hair which Sergeant, or Drum Major, Longrey brushed. The silk of her *ao dai* fell to midcalf front and back. Under this, she wore white silk trousers.

"The thing with this flower, this orchid I got here, Corporal . . . it's more than sex," the drum major said. "At my age you can't keep on with that forever. Don't get me wrong. I've got family, my wife's lovely. I'm here on a second tour by design. I'm a seeker, sort of an American accordion imperialist. My wife worries, but it won't be long and we'll have this won."

"Yes, sir, we will. I'll be relieved to be out in a few days and home, too. I'll see friends, go to school, straighten out my mind from all this."

"You going to learn your music? You going to take out that cotton?"

"Yes, sir."

When the drum major removed his glasses, the housekeeper touched them gently to her tongue, then returned them so he could polish them himself. He paid her one hundred piasters to do this. When he whispered again he handed them to her for her to place on his dreaming face.

"*Vien au lait,*" she said.

"*C'est Si Bon,*" he said. Then, to Vankiewicz: "It's a good song. Tomorrow there's other music." Pulling on his accordion, he walked out the door with her, past the tents, past the lister bags which held drinking water, past the motor pool. The drum major's hair and eyeglasses shining in the sun, Vankiewicz watched him march down the road, accordion hanging from his chest like an instrument of war. In her rush to keep up, the housekeeper followed a step or two behind, the white *ao dai* flowing about her legs. How much had she been paid to love the battalion drum major? wondered Vankiewicz. From the sandbag listening posts along the perimeter of the compound you could hear his music dying out over the din of birds and insects. Melodies like wisps of cloud occasionally floated back, then were lost in the tropical air.

When the drum major returned at 1600 hours, Captain Shaeffer asked his advice in love. Second Lieutenant Frodeson, fresh from Quantico Officers' School, laughed approvingly at the accordionist's *amours.* Maybe longing for a different life had made the drum major return to Indochina, thought Vankiewicz. Maybe the accordion imperialist needed a war: the incongruity of bamboo, elephant grass, snakes, and accordions would help the drum major leave his mark on this country in the way Americans had for years in Korea and the Pacific Theater. Back home nothing about accordions was political. At the Kosciuszko Fraternal Club or Belgian Hall where Vankiewicz ate with his parents on Saturdays, the polka bands were loud, the people happy, but here . . . the drum major was making the Republic of South Vietnam an accordionist protectorate. It was a wide world opening up to the excitement of accordions, and this new world was all going to be the drum major's, thought the Corporal, who himself wished no part of foreign travel.

* * *

Like a dream now, every day the Sergeant Major's housekeeper would appear under the awning of the tent. Near 1100 hours when Vankiewicz and Private Borski returned from their breakfast patrol to the dump, she would retire inside from sewing or washing the drum major's clothes. Evenings when he came in from the jungle, there she'd be under the awning, back before him.

One day, the sixth before Vankiewicz left Vietnam, he saw her sitting with the accordion.

When the drum major, the neocolonialist, said "*Vien ici,* put it down," she did. The hair he stroked and brushed as he hummed ran through and around his fingers. How beautiful she was! Vankiewicz thought . . . like the women who strolled past the old French villas on the Avenue Pasteur in DaNang, while in another part of the city one-armed beggars and street vendors crouched along the walls outside the DaNang Hotel.

"Sing," the drum major said to her when he quit brushing her hair.

She laid her head against the door frame of the tent.

"'Twist and shout' . . . 'Work it on out,'" he said, fingering the chords on his accordion.

"'Twis' an' shout'," the housekeeper said. Then she stopped, looked at her feet in the thongs the Vietnamese made out of old tires, and asked, "Honey, you go out tonight?"

"I'll play 'The Waltz You Saved for Me.' I'll play it all night. Who's on listening post, Vankiewicz?"

"I am, sir."

"Be fun to be outside at night, don't you think? It's a crazy war. You'll have to tell us how we sound. It's the *Ngu Hanh Son.* Pacify 'em or kill 'em. You're doing your part too, Corporal, dumping our garbage all the time. You gotta look up my

wife. This new one I'm teaching musicianship and the excitement of accordion to. Hell, I might go AWOL."

"Yes, sir. She's an orchid."

"She's that. She's got talent, I tell you, Vankiewicz. Hell,
you can get sex cheap, but this is political philosophy. I start
here, pacify villages with the accordion. I want 'St. Louis
Woman' drifting over the elephant grass . . . 'Blue Skirt
Waltz' ringing in the lunar New Year. I want Buddhists to
dance. Where do I start but with people like her. Pay her a little
attention, brush her hair. All this ancient warlord nonsense,
when they really need accordions. There's an old Vietnamese
saying: 'The writ of the emperor don't extend inside the village
gate.' Where the emperor can't go, I say the accordion *can*.
Who don't like 'Maria Elena' and 'Blue Eyes Cryin' in the
Rain'?" the drum major said, adjusting his wire-rimmed
glasses. "These things keep rubbing back there I'm gonna get
an ear infection in this heat. We'll be out to see you later,
Vankiewicz."

On the old Mandarin Road that runs past the Esso terminal at
Lieu Chau, then runs all the way to the Imperial City of Hue,
Vankiewicz watched them striking off into the bamboo grass.
By 2300 he could hear accordion stylings; by 2400 hours,
midnight, vocal accompaniment. By one A.M. of the new day, a
firefight had broken out far south, tracer rounds going back
and forth, but it was so distant Vankiewicz couldn't hear anything. From the northern sector, however, beyond Number 4
post a kilometer or more away where the imperialist had gone,
a duet rose up in different keys. In the jungle night beyond
where the Trans-Vietnam railroad ran, Vankiewicz and the
Marines could hear "To You, Sweetheart, Aloha" and "Nea-
politan Nights."

"Halt!" he said when the musicians returned at 0300
hours.

"It's us. Who else would use the accordion for counter-terrorism?"

"Proceed, sir," Vankiewicz said.

In the morning when Vankiewicz crawled out of the tent, the Sergeant Major was already directing the band in the tropical sun. "We'll take it from the top," he was saying, standing on an ammo box under the parasol, tapping his baton, raising his arms.

In the quiet tent another voice rose to the soft opening and closing of an accordion, which, with its bellows and reeds, is not an ignoble instrument. "Go—finger. He the man . . . the man wi' the Mida' touch," she was singing, smiling, working her fingers over the bass buttons. Vankiewicz sang with her. Soon he could stare at Lake Superior and forget the music he'd heard and the old people who'd swum upstream into the food. Thirteen months of VC in black silk pajamas, Marines tossing equipment into outhouses, garbage dumps. It was time to say goodbye to the xylophonist and the Second-Looie.

"I've written my wife," the Sergeant Major said when Vankiewicz had two days left. Then a day later, "*Sayonara*. I have rehearsal." He gave Vankiewicz a laminated photo of himself in dress blues, arm around the accordion; below the picture, an advertisement from the *Superior Evening Telegram*.

VFW CLUB TONIGHT

ONE NIGHT ONLY

MARINE SGT. MAJOR

CARROLL LONGREY

AND

ACCORDION

"It's a keepsake. Got it when I was home. I gave my Mrs. back there your address. Stop and visit."

"I will, Sergeant Major," Vankiewicz said.

On the way out, the driver took him by to see the old people who'd now built model homes of tin cans and cardboard among the rats. *"Au revoir,"* they called. Across the rice paddies he saw the band, too. With tubas, cornets and drums—though no accordion—they marched single file. Waiting in the woods at the edge of the rice fields were probably ten times as many men, Vankiewicz thought. From high up in the MATS jet flying east for the Bay of DaNang and South China Sea, then east toward home, he could see the band looking as though they'd become disoriented, as though the student of war had made them stop at the edge of nowhere while he cleaned his glasses and taught them the music of *Pajama Game.*

III

"Son, son," his aunt said when he arrived home. Her breath was white in the cold shed. "Your father's so happy you're back. He's got this new hi-fi, this radio. He wants you to join him down at the VFW for a beer."

"Tell him I was tired. I'm going to sleep, Auntie."

When the Corporal heard his father coming in later, he did not go downstairs, nor did Mr. Vankiewicz come up, thinking that tomorrow would be soon enough to debrief each other on wars home and abroad. After four o'clock in the afternoon when the debriefing never came that day, Vankiewicz for his own safety set up a listening post in the room so no sudden noises could startle him. He'd come fourteen hours out of the dark, spent four days being processed at Marine Air Station–El Toro, then another seven hours to get home. A day later he walked to Hammerbeck's Coffee Shop, then to the shore where the temperature was a hundred degrees colder than in Vietnam. The waves there formed ice cliffs—listening posts where you could hide out and await the drum major. The Viet Minh in the old days, the North Vietnamese Army, the Viet Cong: they were all crazy fighting the Chinese, the French, then us, thought Vankiewicz. They never quit either. Even in Superior with its ruined downtown, bleak, frozen streets, and Left-Handed River they kept fighting you.

There'd been a telephone call, his aunt said.

"Hello?" he said when she called again.

"Hello?" After the woman repeated it and Vankiewicz didn't answer, the voice on the other end rose. He could hear a child screaming the way he'd heard gooks scream when Phantom jets flew in low over the Annamites which drop down to the Bay of DaNang.

"Welcome home, GI," she was saying in that squawking, singsong language Vankiewicz had heard for thirteen months. "Ask about husband."

"It's Vankiewicz. Can I come and see you?"

He brought with him a newspaper clipping his father'd saved of Colonel Ngoc Loan blowing out the brains of a VC suspect. In the singing dead of winter there was nothing in Superior, no fatherly advice to quiet him, no resin, seed or stem of home, Vankiewicz thought, just the highway to the Vietnamese wife sixteen kilometers away. The tanks nudged back the darkness and the snow. He thought of how two weeks earlier he'd been listening to the band in the rain, booking shows in Tien Sha.

He'd seen the house in a photo Sergeant Major Longrey showed him, the small white bungalow at the end of a drive.

"How he look?" she was asking when she met him. She had large dark eyes, smooth skin, an altogether beautiful, delicate face. Down her back fell straight black hair like the house-keeper's. She held her shoulders very straight, too, the way these women of privilege had the habit of doing.

"Husband all right? How he look? We marry one year," she said, inviting Vankiewicz to a couch. In one corner stood an oil furnace that came on periodically. "We have son who asleep. Son have privileges he no have in Ve'nam."

"The Sergeant Major looked fine," Vankiewicz said.

"Ve'nam very pretty country. How you like States again?"

"Lots of snow now," Vankiewicz said.

From a stack of papers atop a phonograph, she brought the Corporal's letter.

"I no listen to music on phonograph. Too much music all the time in America," she said.

The letter had been postmarked two weeks earlier. "Dear Vankiewicz," he'd written:

I'm calling it "Accordionaville." You've never seen the like. How's my American Mrs. look? Have her show you my record collection. She's a POW for our side. By the way, I may desert. God, how fertile this Asia.

Yours in truth,
Goldfinger

"This one's Miller. This drummer's Dye. Here's the trumpeter Howie," Vankiewicz said, showing her the photo the drum major'd sent.

"What he say to you?"

"Says he thinks of you. Told me you shouldn't worry."

She sat by the couch in a chair with worn armrests. The dark house with its inexpensive room heater and wood paneling was like a cottage where vacationers came every couple summers to relive the past.

"*Tuyêt dâý sân,*" she said, reading from her own letter to the Sergeant Major.

"I don't understand your language," Vankiewicz said.

"My husband have someone read for him?" she asked, rearranging her *ao dai*. The white silk lay like snow against her almond skin.

"I don't know," he said.

"Husban' no good away. Wish he here. America *beaucoup*," she said. "We marry only one year. I wait long time. He have someone? Ve'namese?"

"I don't know," the Corporal said. "He'd come from being home here. He got there when I was leaving."

"He different? Sergeant Major changed?"

"No different," Vankiewicz said. "Seemed *beaucoup* to me like anyone else."

The drum major's house stood in the south range of hills outside Superior. From the window Vankiewicz could see the radio towers spreading out over the night skyline like a platoon. She was setting out teacups under the dim kitchen light. It was going to be different, this homecoming, he thought. But they always kept fighting you, even here. Even the magnificent Goldfinger's wife might be one of them.

In the next room the child must have taken chill or heard the American. The Sergeant Major's wife brought the baby in crying. She laid him on a blanket on a bamboo floor mat.

"Six mont' old. He taken care of in United States. I wait, expect husband. On tea plantation I wait too, all day long. Then I go to work for him in Ve'nam. He all the time accordion," she was saying. "We also have song. *'Duong truong tai luong,'* song of sadness tells our hopes. Song t'ousand years old."

He hadn't seen the instrument on the floor beside the couch. The *dān tam* had three strings. When she struck one note, then another, it was as if Vankiewicz remembered what longing was. The Sergeant Major's wife sang the old song as though waiting for her lover by the Mekong or the Song Huong, as though her lover wore black and crouched with others at the edge of a tunnel. Even here they fought you. What had he, Vankiewicz, been waiting for all these months? he wondered. What was there to expect in his own village?

Perhaps he could study the reed organ family. What other instruments were in this family? What if you expanded the bellows of accordions? What if you kept expanding and expanding them till you found just the pitch that broke your heart? The Sergeant Major would be marching the band, the housekeeper singing "Go—finger," but here in the North, no more than ten miles from the house where he himself was born, sat Bac Phàm, Corporal Vankiewicz beside her. The drum major knew his show tunes all right, thought Vankiewicz, *Guys and Dolls, South Pacific, Brigadoon,* music as soothing to the senses as a waterfall. So did the city know its music. The radio towers marched along these hills so people from other countries could hear the music of the Western World.

"*Dàn tam,*" she was saying, "We ha' *nhi môt* too which have two strings and *nguyêt* which is 'moon-shaped lute.' We have 'rice drum' and 'bamboo flute' and *dàn bau* and *hô trung.* On Ve'nam tea plantation I walk all day, pick the white leaves, and sing to myself. Now you play it," she said. She listened as he struck one note, then another. The music hung in the air as it had for a thousand years.

By now the boy was sleeping, his dreaming begun. Maybe his father wished to sit opposite the VC in district hamlets or in the tunnels beneath playing the old favorites, the Corporal thought. Vankiewicz, who himself had stopped playing, put down the *dàn tam.* There were expectations, and they were always sad, he thought. Neither Bac Phàm nor the Corporal wished for much anymore. They could sit together on a couch now, watch the snow, and stare at the portrait of a man far away who loved music, a drum major who'd gone too far beyond the listening post.

After a while there was just the snow outside and the oil stove inside—the wood paneling of the living room, the green carpet, the old couch and chair, Vankiewicz's low voice recalling coming home.

"I get here. What's home?" he was saying. "It's winter. I been dreaming about coming out here, expecting things."

When he touched her arm he was surprised that she didn't move.

"Now I wait long time," she said.

"He talked about you. I was there. He was performing 'My Melody of Love.' Bobby Vinton. 'The Polish Prince.'"

"Wait long time," she said.

"I come home. What's home?" he said, taking the cotton from his ears.

"*Beaucoup* States," she said.

"My skin's so dark from the sun over there," he said.

"No dark. *Beaucoup*," she said.

He was running his hands over the silk of her *ao dai* the way the Sergeant Major must have. Across her forehead ran a tremor, like wind over the water of the sea he'd crossed.

"*Tuyêt dây sân,*" she was saying, her beautiful, dark fingers running silently across her lap.

During their struggle to keep from expecting too much the child on the floor slept. The Marine and the drum major's wife were both very modest. She'd waited a long time by the River of Perfumes, the Song Huong. According to the song she played on the *dân tam*, she'd spent a thousand years waiting. Outside they heard no music but the snow, which flew like rice chaff against the window.

The boy was sleeping. The music had quieted him. She put him in the next room. Her own bed was there too.

"No dark . . . light skin," she was saying about the baby as she pulled back the comforter of her bed.

As she undid her *ao dai*, the baby slept in its crib. It was so dark in the room, Bac Phàm herself so dark, that momentarily, when she whispered her language to him, Vankiewicz thought she, Bac Phàm, heard from far off in the jungle the drum major or the housekeeper or someone else she was thinking about. This was only momentary, like the blinking of lights on a tower. Then they struggled in the dark with each other's hands, each other's arms, struggled, it seemed like, a thousand years.

While the war was going on, he would visit her tomorrow again, Vankiewicz thought, maybe take her to town. What with the war, such things happened where people became prisoners. She'd have to stay here in the land of snow and ice with her son, her music, her memories of orchids that grew in the jungle. In Superior, Wisconsin, thought Vankiewicz, who knew more about war and the memory of orchids than the drum major's delicate wife? And in Vietnam, where there was no snow, who knew more about love than the Sergeant Major?

The Perimeter of Light

OCTOBER 17

E VERY fifth round looks like a tube of lipstick. At night the red lines of your tracer bullets show you where your fire is directed. When they ricochet off a rock or a piece of metal, the red lines continue until the rounds die out—spent in the heart of the beast, you hope.

When there are no firefights you listen all night, which is fine. No one wishes to engage the enemy. Sometimes he slips past. At home he wins hearts and minds. At dawn on the way in, marching single file, you're too tired to laugh about the night.

OCTOBER 20

A Marine finds himself illuminated. He has no idea who sends up the flare at midnight. Out of vanity he remains standing when it explodes. It is possible during precisely that moment on the 20th that he is the most illuminated Marine in the South Vietnam "I Corps." It bothers him: he thinks some agent or agency, or perhaps his friend in the bunker, has set off the flare to make him appear foolish and vulnerable. He is too young to have such moments, yet they return.

Later that night, or perhaps it is the 21st, something else happens. Private Edward Zimski, the illuminated Marine, finds a naked man kneeling by his bed. It can't be a moment before the figure is gone and no one knows who it is. Private Zimski lies awake. Was it a dream? he wonders. He listens to the men breathe. Securing the mosquito net, he finally falls asleep. In the morning he looks about. His ammunition clip is there, the flak jacket, the M-14 loaded with tracer bullets.

"Here," he answers as Platoon Sergeant Reed calls his name in morning formation. (The Marine Corps has been good to Private Zimski and his friends, Johnny Wilson and Benny Wicklund. The Corps has done wonders for them, and they have seen wondrous sights. But nowhere in any of the posters or literature of recruitment has anyone said anything about a man by your bed.)

OCTOBER 23

Benny Wicklund, one of Zimski's friends, shoots himself in the foot with an M-14. Wicklund has bright red hair, a red freckled face, and a red eyebrow. His other eyebrow is white and curls like a snowy sideways ∿ . They call him "Lazy S." For fun, he tries dyeing it with red ink. He is from somewhere in Iowa. When Private Zimski returns from picking up classified messages one afternoon, as he hurries across the footbridge by the bunker, he sees Wicklund propped on a stretcher, looking around. "Where we off to, Benny?" Zimski asks. Wicklund's face is white, as though he's seen or heard something terrific. His eyebrow is a little whiter than the rest of him. He stares at things around him and doesn't respond.

"It's the worst thing somebody could do," Johnny Wilson says later on the 23rd.

"He wanted out, I guess," Sergeant Reed says. "So he shot himself. Anything to get back to Iowa."

The letter Wicklund got was written in green pencil lead:

Benny, it's bad. I can't believe it. I've been to see your Mom. I didn't tell her anything. I just got my pictures and left. She asked me what it was about, what was wrong. I didn't have the heart to tell you last summer. I never thought I'd hurt you. I don't feel the same way about you. I can't wait. Mom says I should enjoy myself while I'm young. No, it's nothing with other guys.

Love Always,
Cynthia

When the wounded Wicklund first crossed the sea in August with Zimski and Wilson, the smell of love changed. Zimski himself thought if you didn't keep in touch with your heart, you'd end up sleeping on mats, or eating rice or dog. You could find yourself transformed. Zimski was perceptive this way.

About Zimski and transformation: he was privy to classified documents. As of November 10 he was a Private First Class, USMC, and held a security clearance which allowed him to see information, usually messages headed CONFIDENTIAL in green and SECRET in red, and coming from JCS, Comm 3rd MarDiv., or equally cryptic sources. He never mentioned the messages. In time they were disseminated to the company:

driving at night with windshield down, a Marine was decapi-
tated by piano wire strung across Highway 1; the Bob Hope
Show with Carroll "Baby Doll" Baker will appear DaNang,
12/3/65; Major General Lewis Walt to make tour of inspec-
tion, 10/20–10/30/65; Troops are cautioned to stay together on work details and liberty since a Pvt. James L. Bass,
who wandered off from 3rd Shore Party Battalion work detail,
9/8/65, was found disemboweled, 9/10/65, in DaNang
River; Marine who bought glass of Coke with ice from female
vendor along road on 10/9/65 swallowed crushed glass.
Troops cautioned to . . . ; following DaNang bars declared
off-limits to American military personnel: Bar New York, Bar
Tokyo. . . .

The message that intrigued Zimski concerned a Westerner
who'd been seen in the hills with the Viet Cong. He was the
leader in two ambushes and also in various sniper attacks
against us, the Marines reported. G-2 speculated on his ori-
gins: perhaps he was a holdover from the French forces and
the loss at Dien Bien Phu. Perhaps he was an American defector. How eerie, they said, to see him dressed like that and fir-
ing back at you. On this day in November, Zimski wondered
which language the traitor spoke.

The private himself was being transformed. Now he had a
river journey to make, a short one, Sergeant Reed promised,
but for Private Zimski in the wrong direction. He was troubled some nights by the man who knelt by his cot—this and
the heat and boredom they suffered and the uncertainty of
patrols and what had happened to Wicklund and what had
happened with the flare. Some nights he could feel the night-
flying insects weighting down the mosquito net until he had
to crawl out in order to breathe. He felt a human figure.
Reaching around to catch his balance, Zimski had, one night,
touched the skin, he'd felt the pulse beat, of a human figure.
The rain slapped down on the canvas tent. He saw a naked

man in the lightning. It could be a dream, Zimski told himself. What could he have done, he wondered, wake everyone when maybe no one was there?

In early December of that year an American comedian came to Vietnam. He brought with him some Playboy bunnies: these and various cameramen and technicians came in by helicopter one Wednesday.

Zimski tells Reed there are messages to collect at the air base. When the helicopter brings "Baby Doll" Baker backstage, she has to hold her skirts against the draft of the blades.

"Look!" Zimski says to himself as he rides past. He takes the circuitous route. Places which entrance the imagination exist nearby. Suddenly, in the hills he's been traversing, such a rich, deep cliff appears that he throws out his cigarette. The cut runs deep into the side of a hill, which is closer to being a small mountain. From back around the bend a few miles you'd never expect to find such a cut. The jungle of trees, creepers, and vines spreads from the base of the hill upward. Beautiful remnants of heaven float like silk among the trees. They bless the earth from the tanks and planes that haunt the country with flame. To Zimski it's like another place entirely.

We got out a few miles, he thinks. *It's like she knew we were coming. She's standing in those shower thongs, the black pants and shirt and round straw hat. All the mess tent leftovers, creamed beef, eggs, toast, all the slop nobody eats, and she's standing right where Mullin backs up to dump it. Mullin lets go. The truck bed tilts up, the tailgate slams open, and she's standing there shoveling it in with her hands, eating and suffocating. Jesus, it's pouring over her. I hate it, man. (Rae-Ann's gonna send a portrait of herself. 'Send lots of pictures of yourself when you're away,' her Ma says. I hock their camera on B.C. Street in Koza, Okinawa. One way or another, if she sends me her portrait, there's gonna be pictures involved.) Twelve of us in a rice paddy. One of those round straw hats they wear, the kind that comes to a peak at the top; she's wearing one. Her teeth are black from betel nut. I dragged her part way. I don't mean to hurt her. She's crying. The guys take off toward the pagoda where we've seen an explosion. God, this is weird country. She's crying. I say 'Don't' and let go of her arm. Once we get out of the paddies she calms down. She must know I mean no harm. I'm crying.*

The dense jungle downshore captures Zimski's mind. He pushes against the weight of water which, on the surface, lies flat and still. He feels a long way from the compound, from someone he thinks may be waiting in the private places, the privies or the storage tent.

No one of the Marines comes this far today. Only PFC Zimski, the illuminated, floats in the South China Sea, struck by the stone temple whose white walls obtrude from the jungle. The others are with Bob Hope. Held close by the warm, gray water, the illuminated Marine finds the pagoda's whiteness troubling him. The temple or pagoda fits into the trees of the shore, as the white mists do halfway up the cliffs. The pagoda's whiteness in the dense, green shore growth draws him to it. Though very gently, he feels something tug his leg underwater. He wants to call out. Here in the gray, threatening water, he feels something touching or pulling his leg. Maybe it is the mind.

Wilson got drunk on Vietnamese rum. We were smoking. He stepped on a nail in the tent. To my friends the sun feels good. They complain of the food, of bugs and dust. They shoot Viet Cong. Wilson scored forty points in a game. They didn't like me in school, he tells us. He brags a lot. He has troubles with people.

(A Canberra Bomber exploded. The Australian pilot ejected. We were in the tent. This piece whirling down struck the ground. We were smoking.)

JANUARY 9

A New Year. The men of the company don't bother L/Cpl. Wicklund about the eyebrow. He returns one day and that's that. What can a person say? Wicklund is preoccupied. He goes about his business, but keeps to himself. He made it to Japan, but they wouldn't send him stateside with his wound. All he got for shooting himself was rest and a return flight to South Vietnam. It appears he has found enough strength in Yokusuka to get through his tour without shooting himself again. They put him in with a different crowd this time. His old billet's taken by men beginning their tour. They don't court martial him in Japan, just fix his wound. "Lazy S" hardly limps. New guys say people in the States protest the war.

A tent for storing communications gear and a couple of four-man outhouses are the only structures empty during the day anymore, and with the outhouses, it's a matter of luck to find one empty. No one staffs listening and guard posts during the daylight hours, but they are hardly private since the tanks cleared the foliage away. Flame, not tank rounds, shot from those barrels. The fire cleared the ground, and you could see someone coming a quarter-mile away.

FEBRUARY 14
Valentine's Day

A PFC Glen Desjardins of Tacoma, Washington, a boy new to the company, has been bothered by someone coming to his cot at night. He's told Sergeant Reed. When Zimski and Wilson talk about things at the washrack, Zimski says nothing about the night in October he couldn't breathe under the mosquito net.

"We gotta get whoever it is," says Zimski.

Desjardins, too, has been having a visitor then, Zimski thinks. When others are asleep, PFC Desjardins has felt the hand on his arm and someone naked whispering.

"Zimski," Wilson says, "don't say nothing around the company, not to Wicklund, not anybody. We're gonna catch him. I think it's a Corpsman."

But the days of February pass and no one comes at night. No Valentines come in the mail either. Machine guns flare up at the perimeter of darkness. Not much happens. The company is promised movies, *Goldfinger* . . . *Cleopatra*, but gets neither. These days movie call comes less often.

Zimski thinks of Superior, Wisconsin, his home. He writes Rae-Ann, telling her how, through the vent in his room, he used to hear his mother, Mrs. Evelyn Zimski, talk over the telephone. Coming up the vent, her voice would get distorted; her laugh would frighten him when he was younger. Rae-Ann had sent her own portrait some months before. He thanks her for it, saying how pretty she is. He hasn't written in a long time and, of course, has sent no pictures. Zimski recalls his upstairs room. He can see the letter jacket hanging on the chair. Superior East High School.

Pvt. Wilson is a curious friend, Zimski writes in his letter to Rae-Ann. Before leaving Ohio, he met a man, an older man, his football coach, and during several nights by the bottling works, they engaged in such things as Wilson never dreamt possible. He told me this, Rae-Ann, that's why I can tell you. The coach explained formations to my friend Johnny. Now coach writes. He's had a losing season, but every week comes a letter, a card, a package of cookies and nuts for Johnny.

L/Cpl. Benny Wicklund, "Lazy S," shot himself for love, Rae-Ann.

* * *

In the vast darkness on the night of March 8, the new man, Desjardins, feels someone stroke his hair. Then he's come, he thinks. "Not here," he says.

"Where?" It is a whisper, a man's low, soft, eager whisper. He keeps after Desjardins's hair.

"The comm tent," whispers Desjardins. It is too dark to see. There is no one awake but Zimski and one other, Wilson. The rain has stopped. Desjardins and the man go quietly between the tents. Only once does the man stop to touch Desjardins, who now sees who has been interrupting his sleep.

Zimski hurries to wake Reed and the lieutenant. There is some scurrying around the compound, a challenge from the guards. Flashlights shine the way. Probably no one in the tents even notices, while in the communications storage tent, lover and loved join delicately to explore their pain.

In the silence of his own group of thirteen again, PFC Zimski dwells on his home in the Polish neighborhood of Superior while someone whispers past. Zimski, once illuminated, receives hazardous duty pay to avoid the language of love.

MARCH 23

Wicklund is at first ashamed, then grows defiant. "You liked my eyebrow. You liked how it felt," he says to them.

Word has spread about the capture of Wicklund. Zimski, the illuminated, is sometimes sad, sometimes happy—but always proud of his work for the Marines.

"I had to keep stalling Wicklund," Desjardins says. He is almost laughing as he tells it. His voice sounds funny, hysterical-like. "We got to the comm tent. He's telling me he admired me. He kept asking to put his hands in my hair. What the hell took you so long to get the lieutenant, Zimski?"

"Did Wicklund want to get up when you caught him naked?" they ask.

"I thought you weren't gonna show up, you guys," says Desjardins.

They look at Wicklund. With handcuffed wrists he slouches in front of the tents. He focuses the white eyebrow like a curse.

"When we shined him he just knelt there fingering his cock in front of Des. That bad foot of his was sore. He didn't want to get up, he just wanted to kneel. He asked the lieutenant, could we leave him so he could pray awhile?" Reed says.

"Wicklund didn't want to pray," Desjardins says.

"He was going right down the line from cot to cot," Reed says. "But what am I tellin' youse for?"

Wicklund stands in front of them staring at the ground. They've shaved his head, not his eyebrow.

"Some of you ladies," says Reed, "some of youse aren't admitting to it, but I know what happened. There'll be no playin' grab-ass here. I can't prove what Wicklund told me about you girls, but I'm watching. I expect he's scum." Reed points at Wicklund. "This man is scum!" Reed yells.

At first Wicklund keeps his head down, then he looks all of them over . . . Zimski, Desjardins, Wilson, the lieutenant.

"You let me, too," Wicklund says in front of all of them. He accuses Platoon Sergeant Reed. "Don't play innocent," Wicklund says.

Reed catches him in the solar plexus before Wicklund can say anymore.

APRIL 1

Pvt. Wilson of Elyria, Ohio, receives three letters during mail call. One is from his mother, one is from his coach, who explains why he prefers to run the option, and one from Benny,

"Queer Benny" they have begun calling him.

"Give me the letter from Miss Wicklund. You keep the rest," Sergeant Reed says.

"No." They are by the outhouse.

"Lemme see. What she saying about brig chow? Are you and Benny exchanging love letters?"

Wilson tosses the letter in the outhouse. "Read it down there, take your time, stretch out," Wilson says.

"I'll have your ass for this," Reed says.

From then on, Sergeant Reed is after Wilson. Out of spite Wilson tapes a *Playboy* centerfold on a piece of cardboard. Over every inch of her, he places strips of masking tape, a number on each. With seventy-three days left, he is a "short-timer." He strips a number from Miss April to uncover her shoulder. He strips a number to uncover her hand. He strips a number to uncover her breast.

One day, April 10, Sergeant Reed makes Wilson stand at attention.

"Say it good and loud," Reed tells him.

"This is my rifle, this is my gun!" Wilson says.

"Louder!"

"This is my rifle, this is my gun . . . One is for fighting, the other for fun. Which is which?" Wilson asks.

"You want more, fuck-up, do you? Get down on your hands and knees!" Reed yells.

APRIL 14

The river runs west out of DaNang. A small launch takes Wilson and Zimski up in darkness. Occasionally, they see lights or the Navy helmsman says something.

Zimski has changed toward Johnny Wilson of Ohio. "Reed told me about the letters from Benny," he says to Wilson.

"Were you one of the queers, too?"

His arms over the gunwale, Zimski, the illuminated Marine, stares at the blackness of the sky. He has had visitors. He has come to admire the jungle.

"You *were* one of 'em!" he says to Wilson.

Wilson has changed.

"Why would he write to you?" asks Zimski. "Were you girlfriends?"

"Nothing . . . no," Wilson says.

You can't see his face as they go upriver. Private Zimski throws out his cigarette. If some peasant, tired from working the rice and dissatisfied with his meal of dog flesh, hears the boat and man as he rolls away from his wife, what does it matter, except that maybe, once more, the country has been invaded by strange men. Fish tug at Zimski's cigarette. The children of strangers have come.

"Why did you do it?" Zimski asks. "I'd never thought you'd do it."

At 2200 hours and twelve river miles into the interior, they encounter light. Wilson shields his eyes. Zimski steps forward in the launch. They can't see the monkeys outside the light.

Except for a forklift stacking ammunition crates, the place looks deserted. Under the bright, huge floodlights, the launch puts in: out of their dreams, a square of light illuminating boat and men, upsetting the hour so it would seem to be daylight. The generators' hum is louder than the motor launch backing into the river. The forklift operators keep at it, stockpiling tank and mortar shells, howitzer rounds, bombs. To them 1200 and 2400 hours look alike, except in daylight you can see the monkeys on the mountain.

Wilson sleeps out in the light. Don't do it, don't invite him to your lean-to, Zimski thinks to himself. Sergeant Reed said it wasn't far, but we came a ways. Zimski stakes down the tent half, digs a trench around it in case of rain. What went wrong? he wonders.

On the night of the 14th, Wilson can't sleep, can't shield his eyes.

Well into the night, someone—a man, Zimski figures—comes to his, Zimski's, tent. He hears him whisper as Benny Wicklund whispered the nights in October when he was walking with nothing on him but the rain. Every ten minutes now, two fingers scratch twice on the canvas. Zimski hears it four times. Halfway through the fifth, his own fingers return the sound. When Zimski draws his nails over the canvas tent, he hears someone outside sighing, hears him sighing.

It is possible, thinks Zimski, that I have wanted to be close to Rae-Ann. The place I am in haunts me. I am on patrol.

APRIL 15–16

At the foot of the mountain where the monkeys live, dust from the men's shovels and from trucks and forklifts leaves the face and hair streaked with dirt and the mouth dry. The lister bag is filled with water each morning but hangs shriveled and lifeless by supper call.

The stockpiling continues. Wilson and Zimski walk guard duty and fill sandbags at the base of a hill where, high up, monkeys jump from tree to tree. Because of the rumors, no one speaks to Private Wilson. They don't tell him when to start or stop work, when to walk guard, or when or who will relieve him. Men in the outpost turn away. The Gunnery Sergeant forgets him. He leaves Wilson's mail on the ground.

They have sixty-nine days. Wilson, who knows how she looks with so little time, had to leave Miss April. Zimski has had a letter from Rae-Ann asking for her portrait back. One day late in April, and late in the afternoon, the Gunny says, "Saddle up!"

They go out along the highway. They pass the ROK checkpoint. The sun has fallen behind the mountain. The floodlights come on. As the men go into the land without engines, they hear the generators' hum. Over their shoulders Wilson and Zimski see the mountain of arms and the forklifts driving themselves crazy. *I could be home,* thinks Zimski, *watching the river from the railroad trestle. I could go to the Kosciuszko Club, eat with my grandpa . . .*

Private Wilson encounters the enemy first. He sees him, fires. The gook disappears. Like that, and he's gone down a tunnel. They radio in.

"Settle down," the Gunny says.

You are frightened. You are comfortable kneeling in the bamboo. It's private, just you, the bamboo, and your heartbeat. Someone out there is chewing something. You can hear him swallow. The word comes whispered down the line: "Get rid of the goddamned gum . . . the gum!" But the swallowing continues. The word goes back up: "It's not ours . . . not ours." Lover, they are so close you hear them swallow.

I could be wearing my swimsuit, spending the day on Lake Superior, going to the Polish Club at night where they let me drink.

They spring at the flank. Aiming, you let them have it. They try to kill you. You're locked in something red and loud. You head across the rice to a stand of trees three miles from the perimeter. Your barrel is warm. You've suffered no casualties. Wilson replaces his clip. You feel him beside you.

"They flood the rink?" he asks.

"What the hell, man?"

"Back home, Zimski. Did they flood the skating rink back in your town?"

"Christ, it's April, Wilson!"

Zimski thinks about nothing. He's gone too far west.

Someone is chewing. You hear him swallow. Wicklund's white eyebrow is safe. Rae-Ann is free. Johnny Wilson is shooting at the man he met in Elyria. You are all playing hell with a spot in the rice. Your tracer rounds converge there. They give you some back. They are never hesitant to return favors. Wilson wrote a Dear John letter to the man back home—no more plays, no more formations. Reed should be happy. In the dark you don't know who's next to you. There's just the darkness, the red lipstick they lay on you. You may never see another April.

The Gunny says you're moving out. He's called for air support. You are marching west in a slow line along the bamboo woods. There exist such places in the west that it is possible a Marine could chew betel nut for the pain in his gums, sit back looking on the mists in the hills and the pagoda, and never wish for springtime on the Mississippi.

You hear it red and loud in the bamboo and feel their love splinter the wood. "Corpsman, Corpsman!"

The radio message is saying you're frightened to send your pictures home.

"What does it mean?" the Gunny asks.

"Oh Christ, I'm hurt!" Wilson hollers.

"Goddamn it, are you chewin', Zimski?" the Gunny asks.

Wilson takes it through the jaw. One in the arm and one in the jaw—he can't holler anymore.

"Corpsman!" someone yells.

"Zimski," yells the Corpsman. "Lift him! Help it along! I gotta get around him."

"No!"

"Lift him, Zimski, lift him!"

Wilson is blown to hell and crying for you, all for love.

"Lift him, I said, Zimski!"

You are quiet, even your chewing is quiet when the flare goes off. What luck finding daylight at this hour of the night.

"No," you say. "I won't help the son-of-a-bitch. He ain't one of us. He's not from the U.S. He's a gook-fucker, a queer!"

You, Zimski, stand up where Wilson is blown to hell. You know something about yourself, too. You can see the bone of his cheek sticking out in the flarelight. They are stunned to see you standing with May just around the corner. No one fires. "Don't abandon your arms, Private Zimski!" the Gunny is yelling. "Summer will soon be coming. April won't harm you again. Think of Superior!"

Another flare goes off. The high, white starburst expands your world of love and illuminates you and your way as you go farther than you've ever been, so far that you see neither moon nor stars, only the white phosphorescence of a bouquet of spring flowers. "Zimski, Zimski, you bastard son-of-a-bitch, we knew it all the time about you," they yell in a strange language. But all you see are the moonlit paths of flowers on the horizon.

Mrs. Burbul

THOUGH everyone remarked how well the old woman looked, Mrs. Burbul would reply "*Nie szkodzi* . . . It doesn't matter" and go her way through the fields. She went because the distances were very vast and wide and how you looked in God's eyes out there didn't matter. As she passed the houses on the edge of town, people would talk about the old woman, saying she looked healthy for her age and probably appeared this way to God in the fields, too.

Not many wished to visit the fields the way the old woman did, though. Water lay across them most of the time, not draining because of the compact clay soil beneath. Here the peat fires burned in places, smoke rising as through a wound. In the wetlands surrounding the town, people forgot their lives. The soldier Vankiewicz, the Indian Gerald Bluebird whom Mrs. Burbul had seen shooting rabbits as a boy, a deaf and dumb man from across the Left-Handed River; each would come out here to forget and be forgotten. The miles and miles of bleak wetlands: no one thought much about them until a biologist came up to Superior from the state capitol to study the area.

For the old woman his report had disturbing consequences. On three sides of town were rivers and on the fourth the lake, but now, he said, water lay deep in the ground, too. The biologist's report announced that below the town were both "subterranean springs" and eight-thousand-year-old water trapped trying to seep through the clay. With the droughts in states south of here, what could keep the government from draining away the water? She envisioned roads and fields becoming dust, pictured her soul withering as the water was drained. Over these wetlands she'd prayed for years. Now she was so sick about what was happening she could hardly eat.

"What do you want?" the daughter'd asked that morning. "Oatmeal?"

"Soup."

"Soup again, Mama?"

Then the neighbor'd come to increase her fears. "I want to show you more on this biologist's newspaper report," he'd said. The neighbor, Mr. Braiden, had been looking for articles on when to plant his broccoli and carrots when he spotted still another water report. "Look, water can't get down through our soil. That's what the report says in the morning paper. 'Flat terrain and clay soils around here make it an ideal place for wetlands.' Here, just look."

Mrs. Burbul did not know about the weather or when to plant a garden, but she knew the wetlands she walked over. Once before in her life land and water planners had come. That time it was on foot and by horse and plane, an entire country stolen. Now when she found it unnecessary to examine her conscience, when she was able to forget what they'd done fifty years ago to the old country, now there was much news again. Water planners were coming to drain the fields and sloughs—water which had helped Mrs. Burbul forget. She'd left her memories in the shallow water and treeless fields of the barrens, and now things were changing.

At noon her daughter went to the priest. Stanisława pulled the newspaper from her pocket. "Do you realize there's water down here, Father, maybe a couple inches below us that, well . . . it's older than Christ?"

"How're things otherwise?" he said.

"Fine, but the water—"

"Good," said the priest, who lived in a dry area of town and had shallow thoughts. The Bishop had sent him here when the Polish priest, Father Nowak, died. The first thing Father O'Donnell did was remove the signs that read "Polish confessions heard this side" from the confessionals. "We speak American," he'd said. "But believe me," he was telling Stanisława, "she's on firm ground. You tell her that." Pulling out the little phrase book, *Say It In Polish,* he tried to tell Stanisława to say "Diving Prohibited," then gave up.

"Give her this holy water," the priest said. "Tell her it'll make her feel better. Tell her . . ."

Father O'Donnell laughed, but when Stanisława returned home the old woman had packed a cardboard box with statuettes of Holy Mary and the painting of the Black Madonna of Częstochowa. She had her scarf and the heavy blue coat and was at the edge of the bed wondering, she told the daughter, whether it would offend God to hang a scapular from her neck as she left.

"Ma, this is Superior, Wisconsin. You're home."

"I want to go," she said to the daughter. *"Czy ty jest zmęczony?"*

"The river's full of ice. It may be spring breakup soon. Let's sit awhile. I've been to the priest."

"I'm in a hurry," Mrs. Burbul said. She had the pockets of her coat full of little glass vials of holy water. The spiritual exercise was good for her, thought Stanisława, who had seen her mother do this and loved her very dearly but who wasn't interested in watching her pour holy water over the fields anymore. "What a curious custom," she'd been telling her husband for years when the old woman walked into the country where the river came from. Mrs. Burbul knew the lowlands and the river floodplains. Thankful to God and to Holy Mary, for fifty years she'd blessed the water in the fields of forgetfulness. "O God," her daughter would hear her say as though her mother's heart were breaking. Then Mrs. Burbul would spread over the bogs and sedge meadows the holy water the priest had blessed. Now the news that it was older, deeper water in the clay than anyone knew made her lose direction.

The scarf the daughter'd gotten her, the dull, brown color of March, covered the old woman's forehead. She had it knotted beneath the chin. She'd buttoned the winter coat and stared out her window.

"Look, you don't have your boots. It's cold," said the daughter. "How can you walk?"

The river was choked with ice. Over the trestle, which ran a half-mile across the floodplain, they watched the deaf and dumb man who worked at Fredericka Mill. They set their clocks by him. He had come from the old country, had lost a brother there just as Mrs. Burbul had lost a father.

"Look, I see Borzynski going to work across the trestle. He's an old *dziaduś*. How much longer can he keep on?" Stanisława said.

Mrs. Burbul was crying, though. How could her daughter know what she, such an old woman, had left behind? In a while Stanisława rocked her mother back and forth and heard in the hours before the spring dusk old stories about a pail, a duck, and a goose. Then the old woman was silent.

"I'm home," Stanisława's husband called later.

"We're here."

"What're you doing?" he said when he came up. When he'd been drinking he was good-natured.

"I wouldn't joke about this. Ma thinks she's going."

"Give her the car," he said.

"Mama," said the daughter, *"O co chodzi?"*

"Jesus, people are gonna say we went bad if they see her walking around in the cold without boots on. *Babusia*," he said. It was the only Polish word he knew. "Where're you heading? I'll take you to the butcher's for your supper."

Mrs. Burbul pulled out a handful of tissues and a rosary from her coat.

"Come, Ma. Finish your soup. I'll heat it up," Stanisława said. Downstairs, she hung her mother's coat. "You can wear it again tomorrow." At supper the old woman prayed as the daughter prepared the meal. At such times with her mother far away in prayer, Stanisława would stroke her hair or pat the old woman's hands.

"These water plans they've got going," Larry was telling them both, "they're going to drain everything in sight . . . that's what the word is. It's going to mean the rebirth of this city, a new age from old water. They're draining us dry. I've got things to do around here to get ready for the future," he said, getting up from the table.

"Idź z Bogiem," the old woman said. "God be with you."
Finishing her beetroot soup, she went up to her room before
Mr. Braiden could come to upset her more. All over, she
knew, were men like the neighbor and her son-in-law who
tried to change the sky you walked beneath. She saw them in
the shadows the moon cast on the walls in her room. If you
looked up, the men would be staring down into the earth as if
to bury you. If you looked down, they'd say you had too much
on your mind, that you shouldn't be thinking so much. "Look
up!" Someday when Stanisława was old, when maybe she too
had had things stolen from her, and Larry and the priest, then
the daughter would walk by herself into the fields under the
moon. But the memory of the old woman would be fading for
her, Mrs. Burbul thought. Then maybe the daughter would
sleep fitfully for how she had not understood the old woman,
her mother Mrs. Burbul, when she was alive years ago.

"It's coming, the day's coming," Larry was saying. "It's
necessary we share the wealth of water. Pure, clear, Lake Superior wetlands. We're going to be famous. They're studying
us close. We got all the water up here they need in Kansas and
other dry places."

The more the neighbor and son-in-law talked, the more they
confused swamps with sedge meadows, the more Mrs. Burbul,
who heard their voices up through the vent, feared the land
would come to dust. It was like before—grand gestures. That
time it was Poland's soldiers. Now they would lose the land
again. What hope was there for a son-in-law like this? she
thought. Both men were fools who hollered all the time. She
could hear them—or was it the priest she heard hollering?

"When I got home, I tell you, Father, she'd packed her dresses
in a sack," Stanisława was saying to him as she led him upstairs.
"It's like this water beneath gets older. And she didn't have on
boots, like she wants to freeze."

"I don't know," said Father O'Donnell. "I could look in the phrase book, try to get through to her. But it's like these old ones, they're different. They got things they just won't talk about. How deep do you have to go, I wonder?"

Sitting by the bed, he said, "Isn't it cold today, grandmother? What a wonderful woman you are." Then he read to her: "Save me, O God, for the waters threaten my life. I am stuck in the abysmal swamp where there is no foothold; I have reached the watery depths; the flood overwhelms me."

When the daughter, promising to be right back, brought the priest down, the old woman blessed the corners of the room. *"O jakie to szczęscie, że Cię, o Boże,"* she prayed before she lay down to dream of water. You never knew how deep it was, how deep the water was. Odra, Czernia, Pliszka, Postemia: these were the lakes and rivers she remembered from the old country, the farm of her brother, how she'd brought water and straw for "Kartuz," the horse. Hearing Stanisława again, she said, "Plotters and schemers they all come. They shoot thees goose on our farm. Then they ask for my father's pail. 'This pail no good to water horses.'"

"I know, Ma. You've told it before."

"They take us into camp. They throw coal and wood when we're tired from working. The cook, he was Polish man, fixed us horsemeat, called us '*swinia*, filthy pig' even though he was Polish man. Everyone in camp is dying. When the guards run off after the war end, we pulled him down, kick him. 'We geeve you Polish swine,' we said."

The priest was drinking with Larry and Mr. Braiden. The deeper you went in the water of memory, the colder it became, thought Mrs. Burbul. The cook's skin . . . the blade of a shovel in his skull was like the blade of a shovel draining the earth. The water would be funneled to deserts of Kansas,

United States, she was sure the water dreamer next door had told her.

"What in hell? We haven't got a pail for her horse," Larry said when he and his wife came up after the party in the kitchen. "This is 1989 Superior."

"She's been talking."

The old woman heard them at the top of the stairs. The floodplain of the Left-Handed River would be dark, the long, wide river so full of ice that led you up into the land where the compass lay.

He had taken off his clothes. He had made her do it, too. The prisoners had scattered. She'd stolen from the cook's filthy pockets the eye of a potato. She'd stolen the compass she'd buried south of the window in the West here where the Left-Handed River runs. God forgive me, she thought.

He geeve potato . . . rutabaga. He geeve me the best of the rotten horsemeat for food.

Though it was almost spring, nothing was alive in America except the river under the trestle, which had started, the old woman noticed, to shoot water up from beneath the ice, streams of water. Ice was a land you didn't get over, Mrs. Burbul thought. The ice on this Left-Handed River came down toward the lake from where a stolen compass lay after fifty years. She had walked up the river ice into the forest once. Along its length, the long white river now moved and the whole earth seemed to move in one direction *and you were naked and his face was cold when he was through. And all for a potato or bowl of the horsemeat soup.*

As Mrs. Burbul's daughter lay in bed remembering Larry saying, "Jesus, look at the river starting to break," the old woman walked quietly in the hall between the rooms, having lost her way.

"Mama, your pot's in your room. You don't have to go downstairs. Why are you sitting up so late?" Mrs. Burbul heard the daughter saying.

"*Nie szkodzi* . . . it doesn't matter. Go to sleep," she said. *Up through the vent she'd heard them all night arguing the serious nature of bogs and rivers.* The old woman, who had a confession, heard the water dreamer's arguments. The priest too had joined to argue about God. She could confess, but not to him, not to the new priest, how they'd beaten the cook. The priest, drunk, was arguing there was no God.

The cook had seen her coming. She'd wanted to take back something for what he had stolen from her. There was a compass pointing west. She could feel the dirty legs through the pockets where the compass was. The others had run off. She was spitting. She'd pulled the hair from the cook's head. The shovel . . . "Bless me, Father, for I have sinned," she was saying in Polish, words which neither Stella nor the priest would ever find in a phrase book for modern readers. "Do you want me to sit in your room with you awhile?" the daughter had asked Mrs. Burbul when the old woman came up for the night earlier.

But now the house was quiet, drained of sound. Sitting on the bed, Mrs. Burbul could dream of how life had once been in the old country before she'd come to America. Everyone else was dreaming of their future—the priest, Mr. Braiden, Larry, her son-in-law. They were going east, west, everywhere in America, but she, directionless, was sitting here alone in the room. There were lines like lines of soldiers along her wall where the moon shone in. That was how life came and went in the fields of America, too, like long columns of soldiers that each night from all directions came after you into the house with the moon.

A Chance of Snow

MY brother and I are playing in our coats. The ground's hard with frost this time of year. Even if he brushes my coat or just taps my shoulder, I throw him down. Sometimes the air rushes out of him when he hits the grass. I say, "Don't do it, leave me alone, *Gacie.*" He hates being called that. It means "drawers." I didn't see any word for underwear when I looked in the dictionary. It goes from "under-valuation" and "under-value" to "under-wood, *zagajenie*^{n}, *gestwina*^{f}," so I looked in other parts for *gadjy* or *gotche* like it was pronounced, then went

43

down the "G" words—*gabczast* ‖ *ość*ᶠ . . . *gabine* ‖ *cik*ᵐ . . .
*gabka*ᶠ . . . *gach*ᵐ. "*GACIE!*" it said, "drawers *pl.*" I looked
in front for how to say Stevie, which was easy. My own name is
Agnes, Agnieszka.

"You and Steven come in!" Mother calls.

Beyond the fields, the sweetwater sea causes steam clouds
to rise over it. It's the largest freshwater lake in the world,
Lake Superior. The sailors call freshwater, sweetwater. Over
the wind we hear it roar in. "Big North Water," Lake Superior
means in Ojibwe.

"Look at the storm over the lake," Stevie says.

"It's like that all the time when water's warmer than air," I
tell him. "Being in fifth grade has taught you nothing."

"It looks like a storm."

"You're really dumb," I say.

I call him our last name when I'm with my girlfriends and
he comes around. "Get out of here, Kiszewski. There's a fun-
gus among-us," I say. It's like being someone else, like I'm no
part of him when I use our last name for my brother.

"Why's it so dark over the lake?" he asks.

"I just told you."

He draws stickmen on the window.

"Get out of the cold," Dad says.

"Close the door, Kiszewski," I tell Stevie.

"Dad, you should see the lake," Stevie says.

"Does it look like a storm?" Dad asks. "Your sister says no."

"Yeah," Stevie says. "It does."

"*Żimno,*" I say.

"Cold, hey?" Dad asks. "Did you get the leaves picked up?"

"Yes . . . Is Cliff coming over?" I ask. They practice
Wednesdays. Sitting at the kitchen table, Cliff playing banjo,
Dad, the new Soprani, they play "Julida Polka," "Blue Skirt
Waltz," and "Under the Double Eagle." They hold band prac-
tice but never play anywhere.

Steven mimics me.

"Agnes, are you still calling him *gacie?*" says Mother. "Haven't you learned?"

"No, I just said 'got him' when I pinched him."

We eat our supper. Ma puts up the dishes. The kitchen is warm. Dad's chuckling. He enjoys "Major Hoople." After Dad reads it, Stevie wants the *Superior Evening Telegram.*

"It's Wednesday. That means Cliff," Dad says. He gives part to Stevie.

In the next room Dad unsnaps the fasteners of the accordion case. He brings the Soprani into the kitchen. Sticking his arms through the straps, he undoes the fastener holding the bellows. He never closes the door between rooms, thinking we like hearing him play "The Pennsylvania Polka" over and over.

Stevie crawls under the table. Dad will play a little of a song then quit. When he goofs he groans and starts over. He does "American Patrol."

"Don't throw out the paper when you're done," Dad says. He keeps playing. Among the headlines, "Harvest Dinner Sunday . . . Elroy Gas Rate Hike Approved . . . Local Elks Host State Rep," he has circled the Soo Passages, which are boats heading through the Soo Locks. Upbound for here, Duluth, or Taconite Harbor are the Roger M. Kyes, Ralph Misener, Sparrows Point, Cartercliffe Hall, Ziemia Opolska, and Henry Frontenac, the Canadian one. The U.S. Frontenac my Dad once sailed was torn up for scrap metal.

It is confining under the table where Stevie's gone. There's always the risk and danger of the foot, yet Stevie goes under. He waits for Dad to arrange his sheet music. He kind of tickles the side of Dad's shoe, runs his finger along the toe, which he polishes with his shirt cuff. "Thank you, Steven," Dad says. When the music begins, so does the foot—up, down, up, down. It taps out "Helena Polka." Stevie times the foot. In and out of danger he slips his hand, pivoting it on the palm. He slips his fingers in and out under Dad's shoe. "Ouch!" Stevie cries. His head flies up. It bangs the table bottom. Dad stops. "We'll put him in the warmest room," Dad says, holding Stevie's hand down with his shoe. "Ow, Ouch," Stevie cries.

"Sorry," Dad says.

"Who we putting there?" I ask. Stevie shakes his fingers, rubs his head.

"Your Dad's got something on his mind," Mother says.

Stevie takes off. The doorbell rings. "I'm itchin' to try a new arrangement," Cliff says. He tunes and strums his banjo. I am angry at the racket and lose track of my stupid brother. Even upstairs you can hear "Lady of Spain." The ceiling blocks it some, but it still comes up muffled through the vent. If I shut the vent, Dad will think I don't like music. He thinks we're fortunate having a great guest artist like Cliff over every week.

I look for Stevie. He's asleep. As long as I can remember, I've been listening to kitchen band concerts. I've had so much experience that even when I can't hear the song clearly through the vent, I know it by their feet tapping the linoleum. I can identify "Beautiful Ohio," "When Your Old Wedding Ring Was New," "Anniversary Waltz," "Meet Me Tonight in Dreamland," "Hoop Dee Doo Polka," and many others.

In three upstairs rooms hang five pictures of Our Savior. Dad has placed Holy Water and Holy Candles in each room. In mine, a small crucifix hangs from a hook on the window frame, and I have a larger cross over the bed. From each side of my vanity I've hung rosaries, and the vanity's six small drawers are filled with prayer books. In the front of one of them is a calendar of the "Great Days of My Youth." Dad has written in it how Agnes Elizabeth Kiszewski made her First Holy Communion May 19, 1974.

We are up to St. Elizabeth of Hungary in the liturgical year. I lie in bed wondering if this year Dad will let us see movies during Advent. I figure not. I hear Dad and Clifford laughing and playing the accordion and the banjo.

The visitor comes the next day when me and Stevie are in school. Dad is surprised.

"Well, I threw my arms around him. Yes, hugged him, welcomed him," Dad says.

We are in the kitchen where the visitor sits smiling and drinking a cup of coffee. "We only met once," Dad says. "I gave him our name and our address. 'Write to us,' I told him. But who'd think he'd ever turn up? I was kidding about putting him upstairs. Everytime a boat's in they go down to the Polish Club. *Bardzo szczęśliwy jesteśmy mieć was znamy,*" Dad says to him.

Here me and Stevie go off to school and everything is normal; the Sisters beat us up to start the day and to get our blood flowing, we learn, we sing, we work arithmetic, they beat us some more, we pray the Angelus at 11:30, then come home for lunch and there's a sailor at our table.

Dad says, "This is my son."

"Yes, Stefan," the sailor says.

"And Agnes."

"Agnieszka."

The visitor smiles. Mother makes tomato soup. His face looks like it was carved of stone. From the jaw to the chin his face looks like the spike Dad uses to help split logs for the fireplace. His hair, eyebrows, and eyes are all dark brown and stand out against the light skin. There is the small, smiling mouth, and the point of his chin. I don't know what makes him seem foreign, but his face is different from ours. His dark plaid shirt is buttoned to the collar.

"*Wy macie ładnie dzieci,*" he says. "You have nice children."

"They're good kids, too. And where are yours?"

When he answers in Polish, Dad says our visitor has no close family left, just some friends in Chicago.

"We're his friends," Ma says.

"We are your friends," Dad says.

"*Takrze,*" says the visitor. He smiles throughout lunch. Dad is amazed. The visitor thanks us for the soup, bread, and coffee.

"Steven, yours is the warmest room," Dad says.

Gacie is just as surprised at the visitor as Dad. All through lunch he minds his business.

Dad says Łukasz has come out of the ocean, sailed up the sweetwater sea, then somehow got here from the docks on Tower Avenue. "He must've practiced in his mind how he'd do it. How do you beat it?" Dad asks. "Łukasz . . . Łukasz."

In school that afternoon nobody knows about the visitor, and nothing like it has happened to them so far during lunch, so they are the same kids with the same experiences as an hour ago. But not me and Gacie. Foreigners are strange in clothes, looks, and language. I don't know all the ways, but I can tell some by looking at Łukasz Cedzynski. The Sisters of St. Adalbert's School are Polish. Many families here are—but they aren't exactly either. They're more American.

I stare at the pictures of old school classes in the hallway during afternoon recess. Some are from 1920 or 1930. The students in the photographs have come over from Poland. I spot Dad's class. Gacie comes by and calls me "Agnieszka."

Mr. Cedzynski is in my brother's room on the bed when we get home. He's brought a duffel bag stuffed with clothes.

"Mr. Cedzynski?" I say. Stevie sits in the chair, looking at him. From Stevie's window you can see the lake. The trees down by it have lost their leaves. The sun has gone under. The trees and bushes look gray. The weather is like this during Forty Hours' Devotion at church.

"Mr. Cedzynski?"

"No *Angielski*," he says, smiling. He throws up his hands.

"He don't understand," says Gacie. "C'mon, Mr. Cedzynski," he says, taking his arm.

Łukasz gets up, slips on his shoes, and goes downstairs. When my brother tries getting him out the back door, he won't follow. He stands watching the windows steam.

"Oh, you want a coat," Gacie says.

"Steven, leave him alone," Mother says. She is baking a ham and potatoes. Dad has driven to The President's Liquors.

We make the evening paper. Mr. Cedzynski and Dad are at the table with Steven setting our places for supper when I bring in the news from outside. The story is on the bottom right-hand corner of page 1:

A sailor was reported missing Thursday from a ship docked at the Harvest States Elevator, according to a spokesman for the shipping agency Guthrie-Hubner. The man, a crew member of the Ziemia Opolska, may be seeking asylum.

The ship's captain called Guthrie-Hubner around 8:30 A.M. The shipping agency then contacted the U.S. Immigration and Naturalization Service. Immigration officials would not comment on the man's status. An agent in charge of the immigration service's Border Patrol called the incident a "very sensitive matter."

Normally, asylum seekers are interviewed by immigration service officials soon after seeking asylum, according to the St. Paul office. After the interview, an application for asylum is sent to the U.S. State Department, which then returns an opinion to the district office. The district office may then decide whether to grant the applicant asylum for a period of one year, pending further review.

The Ziemia Opolska was scheduled to leave Friday night.

We were excited about the newspaper. "Keep all this to yourselves," Dad says. As he pours their drinks, Dad reads the article to Łukasz. Our visitor looks preoccupied, though. He sips vodka, stares at the newspaper photo of the *Ziemia Opolska*.

I've seen his face in pictures at school, I think to myself. I've seen the rough hands hanging from the sleeves of the students in the photographs; all the boys in their suits lined up and Father Nowak in the middle. Some were born in the U.S. but most of them in Poland. My Dad learned English when he got here. Me and Gacie are the opposite and cannot get away from English. I figure at least some students in the photographs missed their birthplace. My grandfathers and all my uncles belong to the Polish Club. Gacie will join when he grows up. Dad has the form ready: "Application for Membership. Thaddeus Kosciuszko Fraternal Aid Society." People still sing Polish carols on Christmas Eve at St. Stanislaus and at our church, so that proves they miss it back there. Things have changed from what they were, though.

Dad has these Polish government bonds. The green and white paper has all kinds of signatures on them and scrolls, and an eagle, which is the symbol of Poland. The National City Bank of New York will pay their value if you bring or send them in. The paper they were on curls up at the edges. REPUBLIC OF POLAND, it says. BOND ISSUE OF 1920. DUE 1ST APRIL 1949. Dad told me a good Pole would never cash them in. It'd be like collecting an IOU from some friend, or more than that, from someone you loved.

Łukasz likes Ma's cooking. He eats well at sea, but not like this, he says to Dad. He tells us inflation is high in Poland, gas rationed, and that you have to stand in line for bread. I have to explain to Gacie in English what this means.

Mr. Cedzynski says, "I will be happy to walk around and buy as much as I wish. I will not miss the sea."

"We have our own sea, Lake Superior," Dad says.

After coffee, they listen to Polish records. Gacie and me do dishes. The sailor gives us two dollars.

I pray for him. My brother is in my room with the many rosaries, but he is sleeping and doesn't hear me. We live in a port city where you hear ships and tugs for eight months a year.

When the *Tribune,* the Duluth paper, comes next morning there's another story about the defector. "Immigration Office Mum on Ship Jumper," it says. Dad reads as Stevie and me eat. Mr. Cedzynski is shaving in the bathroom and humming some tune. More officials will be coming when we're in school. I want to see how they look.

"The paper says you're in the area, Mr. Cedzynski," Dad says. My Dad is happy. "'The sailor has asked Immigration and Naturalization for asylum,' Did you know that, Łukasz? *Ty jeśteś słynny.* You're famous."

When Dad reads the next part, "Odds appear to be against it," he puts down his coffee. His voice sinks. "Seventy-five percent of the Polish Nationals who sought asylum in this country were denied that status last year," he reads. "'The sailor must show he is fleeing persecution based on race, religion or political affiliation,' said George Wenzel of the Immigration Service. 'The burden of proof is on the person seeking asylum.'"

I read the rest. At the bottom is a chart with the number of people who have applied for asylum from different countries in the news. In the past five years, 8,993 Polish people applied. They only approved one-fourth. There is another picture of the *Ziemia Opolska* in the *Tribune*.

"Guud morning," Łukasz says when my brother comes in.

Gacie says in Polish, "Good morning."

"Nice morning. *Je słysze jak ty się modlisz,*" Łukasz says to me.

"He heard you praying last night," Dad says.

I like Mr. Cedzynski. The thought never occurs to me that Mr. Cedzynski might have to go back when he is trying his best to fit in.

The next Wednesday Cliff rings the doorbell.

"Say hello," Dad says.

Cliff is surprised to see anyone. Stevie sits beside Mr. Cedzynski and shows him his Flute-o-Phone from school, which the Sisters have us buy for music. When Cliff and Dad start tapping out "Helena Polka" again, Łukasz tries following on the plastic flute, but he can't get it and produces only squeaks. Gacie crawls under the table. I'm glad Mr. Cedzynski heard me praying. He is trying to fit in by doing what he can. To try to look more natural, he doesn't button his top shirt button.

Though it takes a week, we get him outside. After his statement to the officials about why he's left ship, he still doesn't feel safe. He wears Dad's coat. I buy him a stocking cap. Sometime now there is a chance of snow.

We hike the ravine. The creek's frozen a little. It's kind of like an excuse for ice and not what you skate on. We walk along the BN tracks, following them across the river to Allouez where Cliff lives. If you turn south and go out, you'll come to a big trestle that crosses the river again, but upstream from where we were. The trestle runs a mile over this partly frozen swamp where beavers and muskrats live. We are up there when Łukasz begins talking. He just starts in like he's doing it to hear himself. Going along the walkway are me, Stevie, and

Mr. Cedzynski. He does all the talking. He is saying, "*Ja proszę abyś my mie pomóg, Bóg*. Please, I hope you will help me, God."

Me and my girlfriends always stop halfway across. Sometimes we see an old woman, Mrs. Burbul, under the trestle just staring at the river. The trestle is pretty high up. In one direction you see white birch and pine trees and beyond, way off in the distance, the Murphy Oil Company with the flame always burning. In another direction is the highway leaving town, the small bridge we crossed earlier, the lake, and more trees and forests. My brother's cold. I stop anyway. I feel sorry for our visitor, Łukasz. We're up high, the wind is blowing right through us when I ask our visitor what's wrong.

His eyes are so rich and deep I believe I see the forest in them.

"Mr. Cedzynski," I say.

I think he wants to tell me right then. I think he tries. But when he starts, the forest goes out of his eyes. I see his tears. He is talking to himself in Polish.

Farther on, we see these delicate spider strands I've seen up there before. They are white and very thin like spider web material, but only individual threads that aren't forming anything. They float along until they catch on something like a guardrail on a trestle. Sometimes in summer you could run up there and these silver spider threads wrapped around you and for a moment made you rich with their silver. When you pull them off a blouse or shirt, they are so light they ride out of sight on the wind. I'm surprised to see any in the fall.

Dad told me a week before that it isn't hard for Poles to come to this country if they have family already here. It is just difficult for those with no one. They have to seek asylum. They can't get visas. A part of one of the spider threads sticks to Mr. Cedzynski's coat after the walk. It is hanging on the kitchen chair. Mr. Cedzynski's face is red from the trestle. By failing to understand, I have let him down, I think to myself.

Him and Dad talk Polish. Łukasz describes things with his hands, sweeping his arms to show something Gacie and I did. "*Czykago,*" he says a couple times.

"He's leaving," Dad says.

I stutter something. Mr. Cedzynski has gone upstairs.

"He'll be back, though," Dad says.

"How will he get back here?" I ask him.

"Hop a bus, I suppose. Sure it's a nine-hour ride, but so what? He won't mind."

They are driving up to get him. I've heard them speak of "Łucya from Czykago" who has telephoned a few times. She's gotten letters from Mr. Cedzynski over the past year. "They left early to get here by noon," Dad says. "They'll be coming."

They hug Łukasz the way Dad did. They shake our hands. Łucya from Chicago has already lived in America, but Michał and his wife have only come over and speak no English. Mother serves them cake and rolls. Stevie and me listen. Once in a while Łucya or Michał say "*Wiele lat ma twoja córka?* How old is your daughter?" or "*Dzieci bardzo szybko rosną.* The children grow up fast." Then they look at us. I am part of the language they speak. When they are talking together and Ma's rushing around the house I don't think I'll miss Łukasz so much. But when he puts on the stocking cap and they pull out in the station wagon, the place seems empty. I never understand why he goes.

I write him in English. I don't ask Dad to translate it because it is personal. I send the spider strand from the coat.

I go back to calling my brother "Kiszewski." I want everything the way it was before Mr. Cedzynski came from Poland. It never goes back that way, though. I think we have to appreciate what's close to us. Gacie needs a new cap. I buy him one.

Sister Benitia encourages me to write about Poland. I even think of asking Dad to teach me Polish.

We have no word from Łukasz Cedzynski. I miss him. The snow falls and covers the path to the creek and the BN tracks and blankets the shores of the great sweetwater sea. Pretty soon, the St. Lawrence Seaway will close down for winter. The last boats have to get in and out. The newspaper says there is another Polish boat, the *Ziemia Białostocka,* upbound to take on flaxseed here and wheat at another elevator.

I don't know what it is to be foreign. Maybe I'll learn when I go to East High. In my grade at St. Adalbert's we only have seven students, Bobby Novack, Antoni Zowin, Jimmy Waletzko, mostly Polish kids, and East is big. Even that's not what Łukasz has experienced, I'll bet. The pictures in the hall tell it. In those faces is a sadness as if the students were torn from something and in between countries. They didn't know whether here or Poland would be better. Maybe I was foreign. I fit in OK, but didn't like kids like Gacie; yet the older girls at East or in the neighborhood didn't have much to do with me.

Łukasz comes back on the bus, and we go to get him. He stands waiting by the Polish Club. *"Ja szczęśliwy ciebe zobaczyć,"* he says and hugs us. He brings presents for Stevie and me. Dad, Ma, and Mr. Cedzynski talk all night. They have a drink or two. Łucya from Chicago sends her best wishes, Dad says. They listen to Polish music. Before sleep I wonder about things. Why did Mr. Cedzynski come? Poland was an old country you talked or sang about. Now with him it was different. He was living proof, an example. You could look at and listen to Mr. Cedzynski and know he was real and an authentic foreigner. Maybe not understanding him was best. When everybody around here spoke Polish, they were still Americans. But not Łukasz. He was authentic. I couldn't wait to see him in the morning.

In the middle of the night, the house grows quiet. At first it sounds like everyone's in bed. I wonder if Mr. Cedzynski is asleep. I hear voices in the vent. It must be past midnight, and someone's still up. Gacie rolls over in bed. Everything upstairs is quiet, just Gacie's breathing and tossing. I see the kitchen light on when I get halfway down the stairs. Dad and Mr. Cedzynski are talking so much they can't hear me coming. They're going back and forth, Dad telling Mom what they're saying.

"Have a drink, Łukasz."

They have water glasses in front of them. As Mr. Cedzynski holds his glass and pours, I stand out of the light to watch. He says something in Polish. He keeps talking as if to the glass, then drinks it down. His hands don't know what to do. The glass teeters as he puts it down.

"Why do you want to do it?" Dad asks.

"*Jest trudno dla mie n . . . ,*" says Mr. Cedzynski before he stops and stares at the wall.

"He grew tired of living there. He had no one in Poland," Dad tells my mother. "He heard of sailors jumping ship in America. He wanted to go and be able to buy bread and shoes and not have to wait for things all the time. There was no reason to stay there, he thought."

Mr. Cedzynski turns his head like he doesn't want them to know he's fighting something. I saw him do that on the trestle.

"It'll help getting some sleep," says Mother.

"You go up, dear," Dad says. But she sits with them, looking tired, checking the clock.

"I think I understand it," Dad says. "There's a tree near his parents' church where they're buried, and two roads cross and crucifixes stand along the road. The crosses are kept sheltered from the rain."

"His parents are dead," Mother says, and Dad nods. "Łukasz misses the stones in the roads around there. He carries a rock from home in his duffel bag."

"He has no living soul," says Mother.

Dad and Łukasz drink another shot. They toast the U.S., and I watch Łukasz fight his tears.

Sometimes in my room at night the wind brushes the windows and they rattle. The snow sounds like rice against the glass. It might have been the wind that made him cry up on the trestle. I've never been away from home, so I can't say how bad a person feels. You see the sweetwater sea from upstairs. On rough, windy nights, you can hear the waves going in and out. Unable to make up their minds, the waves also leave you wondering about everything, about human beings. If there could be a place, some special one in the middle of the land where people were happy and not drawn back to sea like the waves, then I think things would be better for everyone. I wonder if Łukasz thinks this too. I guess I'm happy staying in my Dad's house and going to St. Adalbert's. If I lived far off, would I miss walking the shore of the lake? I wonder. Would I let it draw me back? I think of the thin, silver strands on the trestle and how they hook on in the middle of their way somewhere else. They are temporary and more precious because of it. Slowly, the lake is freezing him in, I think, and I'm happy and fall back to sleep.

The next afternoon, Mr. Cedzynski, me, and Stevie go uptown. After school he meets us at the corner by Hammerbeck's Coffee Shop. It's fun showing him around. I let him put in the bus tokens. We walk to the wide seats in back. Mr. Cedzynski puts an arm around Gacie. Maybe Mr. Cedzynski has forgotten what he was telling himself on the trestle, I think. The bus starts and stops. The Onaway Club, Hayes Court, the sign for the Blue Star Highway go by. We pass the Red Owl Store and the college, people getting on and off.

"Mr. Cedzynski, you see the drive-in restaurant? We go there sometimes," Gacie's saying. "See that cathedral? Sometimes we serve Mass for the Bishop. They have services when the Knights of Columbus wear these things like sea uniforms they got off ship. You see the place in there? It used to be a plumber's. There's the Capitol Tea Room Dad took me to once . . ."

He's rattling on like the wind on the windows last night, and Mr. Cedzynski is nodding and smiling, pretending to understand.

I never know how close to the next corner you should pull the cord to get off. The bus slows down by the Labor Temple. Gacie's still talking away.

"Where would you like to go?" Mr. Cedzynski asks in Polish, but I understand because of how he says it and moves his hands.

"Bouchard's," Stevie says. The owner goes to St. Francis Church out by our church. He shakes everybody's hand when you come in. Wiping his own hands on his apron, he shakes yours and asks how you are. He makes his own chocolates in the back room.

Right away Mr. Bouchard knows Mr. Cedzynski's a foreigner. Mr. Bouchard says, *"Dzień dobry."* Łukasz waves. He buys us licorice. As we eat it he walks between us on the street. He has the stocking cap on and Dad's winter car coat. A shiny, brown sports coat Mr. Cedzynski brought from the *Ziemia Opolska* hangs down partway under the car coat. People stare. I guess you see when someone's foreign. They can tell he doesn't fit here.

When we come to a phone booth on 12th and Tower he checks his pockets. Gacie hands him a quarter. "Mr. Cedzynski," he says.

"Tank you, Stefan."

Right then, I hope Poland isn't on his mind, that he wouldn't know how to call anyway.

"Don't call, Mr. Cedzynski," I say. I don't know what gets into me. I'm afraid to pull a cord on a bus, but I can say that.

I look at his clothes and face and see that he looks lost on an American street.

In the morning it's really cold, the first morning to go below zero. Dad and Łukasz drive us to school. I'm proud to have him see the school. Over the door, carved in the stone entryway, it says: *SZKOŁA WOJCIECHA*, St. Adalbert School. Before I go in my room I give Stevie the money for the hot lunch which we have once a month. I bet him the ice in the harbor will freeze and trap Mr. Cedzynski all winter.

I see Gacie again at noon. He wants more money. In the afternoon when the sixth and seventh grade classes study reading, I ask Sister Benitia to be excused. She lets me read from the bookshelf in back. I read some and look out at the great sweetwater sea. During their conferences, Sister told Ma and Dad I was a good student but a dreamer. I was always off dreaming somewhere. The one book I've been looking through is about Poland. In one of its pictures, the land is flat and green, the road trampled from the many visitors to Częstochowa. In another one, these mountaineers, *górali*, men who live in the High Tatra of southern Poland, are dancing. They wear colorful clothes. I look at their dancing and think of Łukasz.

When we get home Ma's crying. Dad is even home. "I went to work. He couldn't have just walked out and caught a bus," Dad says. "He must have gone somewhere, though. Maybe . . . I don't know. He left his bag."

We drive around to the trestle, then down 5th Street to Belknap the way the city buses run. We turn down Tower Avenue. We check the Kosciuszko on Winter Street and look in the Greyhound Station.

It's a big town, pretty spread out. Where would he have reason to go? Dad wonders. We check a few stores along Belknap and Tower. We stop by the phone booth. "He wouldn't be in a tavern, I don't think," Dad says. Dad drives an hour. By the library, by Bouchard's, by all my relatives' houses. He checks the whole length of Ogden Avenue, Weeks, and Banks. He goes down John and up Hammond. He looks on Catlin and out by the refinery.

The docks are something if you've never been there. The roads get pretty bad by the docks. They're full of potholes, and you have to cross all these tracks. We've got about thirty docks or more in town where they ship out coal, ore, and wheat. The docks have different names: Hallet Coal Dock, Farmer's Union, O & M, Allouez Ore Dock, Great Northern 1 & 2. Dad says maybe we're the twelfth or thirteenth busiest port in the country. In spite of the sign telling us to KEEP OUT, Dad drives up to one of the docks down by these old warehouses and fish packing places. At the bottom of some huge cement elevators like grain silos is a narrow place to walk. If you stepped the wrong way you'd end up in the water. Dad, me, and Stevie head out toward the ship, dirty water dripping on us from the elevators. You can hear the ship's engine. Pigeons flap around us.

"Hurry," Dad says.

The boat is huge. The smokestack and wheelhouse, the ropes and holds are almost as big and high as the elevator she's leaving. Except for the name in white, the steel hull's black. Then right at the top, several thin white and green stripes run the ship's entire length and, very high up on the bow, a Polish eagle is painted in white. Its wings spread wide. Two harbor tugs move into position around her. Some sailors are hauling up the ladder. As men work on deck, there's a banging like they're closing the holds. Grain dust forms a scum on the water. It's also on the ice and on the snow. A sailor looks down from a place above the eagle.

"We're looking for Łukasz Cedzynski!" Dad yells up.

The sailor cups his hand to his ear. He's a long way off. Dad yells again.

The man yells down.

"Yes, Łukasz," Dad says. "We must speak with him. We wish to tell him something."

The sailor yells for us to wait. He disappears. The *Ziemia Białostocka* eases from the dock.

"We can't stand here," Dad says. We head out to the end. The sailor returns. He hollers down above the engines. They are fifteen feet out. He waves, shakes his head.

"Is he aboard?" Dad yells in Polish.

The man nods but hunches his shoulders as if unsure why Łukasz won't come up.

He is leaving, I think. Gacie is crying. There's ice in the harbor, but the tugs and the *Ziemia Białostocka* push through, leaving dirty broken piles. Slowly the tugs bring her into the harbor. We go back down the walkway, Dad hurrying Stevie who can't stop waving. "We'll watch out the entry," Dad says. He's sad. It's getting dark. Cliff will be coming over tonight.

A long, high bridge crosses the harbor. Over the guardrails as Dad drives we see the *Ziemia Białostocka* edge out far below. In the harbor, other ships lie at anchor. You can see two or three miles up the river that makes the harbor.

"He didn't have to. They weren't even coming to his case for four months," Dad says.

We race after Łukasz as though we could reverse what he's done. On the other side of the bridge, we lose track of the ship where the pulpwood and coal are piled up so high on Railroad Street you can't see. There's another bridge. When ships go out a bell sounds and traffic stops. We're there in time. Dad parks on the street. We run through the cold to the entry. The Army Corps of Engineers has trucks and equipment all over. We have to duck around it all.

The ship turns into the entry. The bridge tender answers her signal with a horn of his own. Traffic stops at either side as the whole center part of the bridge goes up into the air. The *Ziemia Białostocka* is blowing her thank you to the bridge tender. Pushing through the channel ice, throwing it up around her, she looks like a haunted dream of Poland in the night. We hear the engines pounding and see the man above the eagle waving. He waves all the way out. We hear the passing, we see the lights disappear, but we can't move, none of us, not me, Stevie, Ma, or Dad, not as long as we still believe we see the lights out in the ice, though they've disappeared.

Some days later, the St. Lawrence Seaway closes. One of the last to get through, the *Ziemia Białostocka* has made it out, the *Evening Telegram* says. Dad checks Mr. Cedzynski's duffel bag. In it are a greeting card and five twenty-dollar bills. *"Niech cie Bóg błogosławy,"* he's written. "Let God Bless You." I spend that night in my room looking at the card in his strange, foreign hand. I look from the crucifix to the rosary to the prayer book. From then on after school I just want to come home and go upstairs to think.

Then the town freezes and there aren't any lake or ocean boats going through. The town and the harbor just freeze over. Even the Coast Guard cutter *Woodrush* is frozen in. My whole life feels like it's ended. Gacie moves back into his own room. He keeps some of his things in the duffel bag. I try writing something, a poem, but I can't even concentrate on homework.

One day late in winter I come back out on the trestle. Ma'd kill me if she knew I went alone. Everything's sharp and white on the earth. The wind whips hard from the lake. Your eyes water and your face feels numb. I think of the times I saw him resting in Stevie's room. When I thought Mr. Cedzynski was sleeping, he was staring at the ceiling, deep in thought, hands behind his head. His dark eyes kind of dreamlike, he'd mutter Polish words.

Now I think about the people who've come here, about their pictures in the school hallway. Sometimes they look haunted like the dream of a ship, placeless and floating. I can hear the bridge bells ringing. What was back there that Mr. Cedzynski missed? What was in the old country that was so special he'd return to it just because of the stones in the road? I wish there could be a place where you forget about everything you loved . . .

Country of Lent

O N Good Friday every-
thing is gray with patches
of snow in the woods.
Out on the sand island, a heron stands in the reeds.
"Lookit," my husband says. He has been drinking. He stum-
bles on the railroad tracks, hurts his knee. The heron glides
forward into the shallows, one leg folded up to its body.
"Look," Gerald Bluebird says to me again.

Two of the herons nest on the island by the abandoned
tracks. They are easy-to-frighten birds. He watches them
climb over the island where the beaver build in the calm,

where herring gulls try out their fishing. He says to me, "You ever seen anything so out of place?" We have come to live where he hasn't been in thirty years.

He wrote two weeks ago on a piece of cardboard. He put the card in the baby's gown: "Baby Girl Bluebird," it read. "February 14–March 31, 1991." Then he started drinking. Upriver there lies our baby. Once in a while I nursed her, but after, when my face was in shadow with the lights off, I felt sick and promised her no more tit. The old woman, the mother-in-law, rocked her, but the baby grew weaker. Now it's the Left-Handed River we hear, Gerald wondering if anybody but us who buried the baby in the box can hear her crying on Good Friday.

"No use," he says later in the house. He has black hair and eyebrows. His eyes, the light brown color of dried hazelnuts, look tired, have black marks under them.

"You're stupid staying in the house," I tell him.

"Where else is there?" he says. He has a dream catcher.

"I don't know. Nowhere." I pull my hair into braids, hold them with turquoise bands. I smear the lipstick in a crooked line. I don't care how I look when the late winter fires haunt me and the aspen sap is bitter. The old woman who lives in the house, she turns down the radio and doesn't read the newspaper, though we know like everybody around what's going on with the white man, *Chimokoman*, who has this thing called PARR to fight us on the lakes and in the woods.

"What's it mean?" I ask him again.

"Protect America's Rights and Resources," Gerald says. "Treaties don't mean nothing to them."

"The love of Christ is in us," the old woman says when she sees us with the beers.

"We're going to church," he says.

"No use staying in the house," I tell her. "We're going."

In the town a half-mile away, the buildings lean over this way and that. Everything's gray. There's nothing in the old town. Some day the Lake Superior wind will push it all down.

"It's Good Friday," Gerald says, kicks a piece of broken pavement.

"The white man come in to drink last night when you were drinking?" I ask him.

"Some of them after church. They line up today, then somebody wipes the lipstick off the feet of the cross at church," he says. "Good Friday. Somebody kisses the plaster feet of the statue."

"I'm not interested," I tell him.

We sit in a booth in the bar. The dark, old place is a hundred years old. The wood floor bends towards the back like Lake Superior waves have come beneath it. On the street are plenty of other bars, the Castaway, the Bolero, Eli's. This is the only deserted one. Since the baby died, I've been in a couple times.

"Nothing come of that baby," Gerald says. He's older than me. Leaning against the back of the booth, he turns off the little lamp. Beer's been spilt on the shade. The floor is sticky under my shoes.

"No baby could've lived in this country," I tell him.

He's wearing his deerskin vest. He looks flushed, dark. The fat guy wiping down the bar puts on a fresh apron and stares out the dusty window. When my husband Gerald is drunk, he sometimes takes the .22 to the swamp to sight in on the blue herons. This afternoon the cross and the statues in the church are covered, everything gone from the box on the altar Gerald calls the tabernacle. His old Ma still worships It. With the blackbirds calling in the swamp and Easter two days away, there's a reminder for things to come back, though no baby.

"How long the baby dead?" he asks. For every day the baby's been gone he makes a ring with his beer glass on the tabletop.

"You want another beer?" Kolanek asks.

"Nobody around this afternoon?" I ask Kolanek.

"Everybody's at church," Gerald says to me.

"You get what you get," Kolanek says. "Try these."

It's a couple cans of Treaty Beer. The white people make it in Minocqua. Use the money they earn to fight us in the courts. The government says we have rights to fish off-reservation. In Article Two, it says, "The Indians stipulate for the right of hunting on the ceded territory, with the other privileges of occupancy. . . ." Now the locals don't let us.

"We don't drink with no assholes," Gerald says.

"Don't drink with yourselves then," Kolanek says.

"I ain't payin' for this piss."

"You'll pay for more than that if you timber niggers go out fishing with gill nets to muck everything up for us business owners. Nobody gonna come to Wisconsin you take all our fish."

"The lakes ain't yours."

At Harmon's bar, the Whoop 'n Holler, we sit in back too. "Give us a couple, Harmon," we say.

Harmon brings us Treaty Beers.

"Beers are on the house," Harmon says and goes back to the bunch at the bar.

"Come on," Gerald says.

We get up.

"You friendly Indians are OK here," Harmon says.

Two beers in the red, white, and blue cans wait for us at the bar. We're the only Indians around. "Drink to show us you're friendly," the white guys say. They look as Gerald pours my beer. "Show your friendliness," they say. "Can you do that?"

"Tastes sour," I say.

Harmon passes down a sheet of paper. "This is *our* friendly," he says. It's wet from the bar—a mimeographed sheet. "Can you draw 'em like this?" Harmon asks. "The fish there holding the spear, that's any ol' walleyed pike out of Cranberry Lake. The squaw there with the big tits and pregnant belly, that's your woman getting speared. See what it says, 'Save a Walleye, Spear a Pregnant Squaw.' It's good," Harmon says. "Whoever made it up, Roy? Pete, do you know? Ed? Go ahead now, you keep that one, Gerald," Harmon says.

Gerald pours his Treaty Beer on the wood bartop. Beer flows in the cigarette burns and settles into the initials carved in the wood. Gerald tips mine over. It flows like the Left-Handed River.

"You really gone and done something on Good Friday," Harmon says, wiping his hands. "You want to just get out of here now." He reaches for his club stick. "You really gone and shown us your friendly." He comes around the men at the bar.

"Leave us alone. We're going to church," I tell Harmon, the bartender.

"No, I wanna show you our friendly," Harmon says. "See how friendly?" Harmon says when he hits Gerald. "See?"

Outside in the dusty wind, Gerald holds his chest and arm. The sign says COME AGAIN. The blue and purple picture blows about in the street. *Chimokoman* was down there on the Left-Handed River last night with his gill nets and metal spears. The white peoples' helmets had lights. The *Chimokoman*, he is not legally allowed to spear fish, but he was down there. In his lights with the moon rising over the river, the birch trees looked sick and white. Gerald pounded in the cross over our baby's grave as we watched everything last night. He brought the two pieces for a cross. He lined them up with the Lynx overhead in the night sky. The moon rose. The white people shined their lamps in the water and speared our fish.

* * *

We go up the avenue. It's full of bars, the Up North Cafe, the Tepee, the Bear Run. It's spring . . . broken glass, dust on the streets. STOP TREATY ABUSE, read signs in the windows. White people write it. PARR writes it. We're the only Indians. Bad River Reservation is ninety miles away.

"Nobody gonna help us," Gerald says.

"I don't know."

"Hell, my arm hurts from where he hit it," he says holding it.

"You shouldn't've spilled the beer."

"Where to?" he says.

We follow the dust. The business district of this part of town called East End has woods on three sides. The big lake where the wind comes up from—there's ice on it, on the shore where the wind's pushed it in.

We pass the Salvage Store, Gerald still holding his arm. Sign over the tarpaper wall says: USED AND SALVAGED.

0° or colder
Free coffee
6 A.M.—10 A.M.

"Cold enough to qualify for coffee?" Gerald says. He writes STOP TREATY ABUSE on the window with his finger.

We go out the sidewalk that follows Raspberry Avenue. The fields, then the aspen woods start and the sidewalk looks like it goes on forever.

"There's marsh marigolds on the side of the embankment on the bay . . . sign of spring," Gerald says where the sidewalk ends.

It comes to a stop in the middle of a field, just stops like the white man got tired and went back to town. Sidewalks like this all over town. Many start like they know where they're going, but crack apart before they get there or end at a tree or curve on to nowhere.

By three o'clock Jesus Christ is dead in church.

"Old woman'll be home now. Nowhere for us to go," Gerald says.

We put up our collars. The fields are all dry from winter. Somebody's dumped a car radiator and a battery out here. It's just fields and distances. The cold, dirty sky whips the grass.

"The baby ain't got a cross except for what we put up," he says. "Priests are no good."

Just the field and the wind. I'm not listening. My belly aches bad where the baby died. "Where you wanna go?" I say to my husband.

"I don't want to turn around."

"Show me your friendly," I say.

"It's too cold to be friendly," he says.

We think about the Treaty Beers, the dead fields, the wind.

"Nowhere much to go," he says.

"How cold do you think it ever got on Good Friday?" The wind hurts my face when I ask.

"You don't see Him, Christ, with much on, do you, no robe, nothing."

"Today he's gone for another year," I say.

"Never did much for Indians," Gerald says, stuffs his hands in his pockets. "Christ Almighty dies every spring. My old Ma thinks He really helped us and was friendly to us. She's praying all the time to Him."

"Pretty cold stuff," I say.

From out here in the fields we can just see the white man back in town. The high brown field grass blows away from us.

"Cold, unfriendly," says my husband.

At the end of the sidewalk the gray sky winds its way to heaven.

"I wish this sidewalk went someplace," I say to him.

"I wish it was warm," he says, "and we were going someplace."

"You're right," I say. "There's nothing here to block the wind."

"It's almost cold enough for free coffee," he says, but he's not friendly about it. He just looks back at the wind.

Old Customs

BUTTERFLIES come to Auntie Pomerinski's garden. They hardly touch the garden vines as they flutter from leaf to leaf. "Some do not wander far from where they were born," my book says. Auntie Pomerinski got it for me, her niece, when I was younger.

The butterflies in her yard are a little yellow but mainly purplish brown. There are small blue spots on them. What you remember are their blue and yellow markings. They are the kind called "mourning cloaks." Along the fence of her yard, I crush grapes in my fingers. All along this fence are clusters of grapes. On windy evenings when the butterflies have taken cover in the garden, I whisper to the wind in the leaves. I am her favorite niece and last to be out in her garden. The direction my voice travels is where Auntie's spouse will come from, an old custom says.

"Marta Davidowski," Ma calls for me. We have been staying at Auntie's to watch her. It's nine o'clock.

"Where have you been?"

"The garden," I say.

Auntie says nothing. She doesn't hear well and can't stand up very long. The veins sink in her arms. She is telling us about a valley of trees near Warszawa where the evening wind blowing through the valley produces a melody which people sing to. Her eyesight isn't good. I read to her from a dream book that says dreaming of a bird's nest means prosperity and honor will follow and dreaming of a priest, that some quarrel will be cleared up. She has cardboard over the front and back covers and rubber bands to hold in the dreams. "It's a sign of happiness if you see a butterfly," I say.

She's begun to doze. Her head falls back. She's old, very thin. Sometimes she says, "I want to go to God now."

"Yes, Auntie," my mother or I will say.

I bring Auntie's bedroom pot to the room. She's left her prayer book open on the pillow. The prayer book's cover looks like it's made of ivory. It has a metal clasp. I have her immigration papers on my dresser: *Be it remembered that Frania Pomerinska who previous to her naturalization was a subject of Poland,* they say.

"Are you tucked in now?" I ask. I lean to her. She is trying to sing about a man who came to America, then returned to his wife and children in the old country.

> Then I left Berlin for Krakow,
> There my wife was waiting for me . . .
> And my children did not know me.

I tell her what I saw. "Do you know, there were all kinds of them in the garden . . . yellow ones, mourning cloaks all over . . . a good dream."

"The last time I dream of butterfly you born," she says.

"I read that to see a butterfly in a garden is a sign of long life, travel, and happiness, Auntie."

"Holy God," she whispers to me.

When the old ones die, they wash them in the house. They wash them very carefully, comb their hair. They keep them in the house and put out the black crepe on the door. On the third day the neighbors come for the rosary. It is an old custom for the men to sit all night before the coffin in the living room, drinking, playing cards. Once, when my folks didn't know I was around, I heard them say, "I'm worried about her. How's she going to take it when her Auntie goes?"

"What are you doing?" Ma calls in the morning. "You've got school."

Downstairs Auntie Pomerinski's staring out the window expecting me home, and it's only 6:30 A.M. I look up dictionary words: dream-*(dri'm) rz. sen, marzenie;* dreamer-*marzyciel, próżniak* . . .

"Tees Polish stuff . . . good, good," Auntie says when she hears me.

When I get to school, Sister is at her desk.

"It's you, Marta. What is it?" she says.

"Nothing."

"Come in." I hear the nuns speaking in the next room. Once in a while I hear my name or Auntie Pomerinski's.

Sister's drawing a holy picture of purple grapes and wheat. "What do you think of it?" she says. She hangs it downstairs in the gymnasium and tells me to go hourly to pray.

At recess I bring my geography book down there to study Europe. Poland, because of its light blue color, looks like a butterfly on the map. With everybody outside during recess, it is just me and the beautiful butterfly country. Through the gym windows I hear the white sheets blowing around on the line where Sister Urszala has hung them. There is a belief that if a picture falls someone died. Sister remembers it from the old country. She's told me to go and wait and pray.

I lay my head back. I dream as Auntie waits at home in the window of the house. She can hardly speak English. She smiles when we talk. I think to myself, if Great-Auntie, who can barely see, never misses Mass, if Sister can paint the Blessed Wheat like this, and if people can hang holy figurines in the streets of Poland to hear them speak, then I should be happy. But I cannot pray for Auntie and doze off in the gymnasium where a light breeze comes in the window.

"Wake up," Sister says, nudging me.

The sun is streaming in, the kids playing. I'll be happy to see Auntie Pomerinski. Hearing me in the garden with the mourning cloaks, she'll wave through the window.

"Wake up, Marta!" Sister says, shaking my arm. "Your Auntie."

I look around. School is quiet. Sister is praying. She takes my hand. The nuns have come outside. I stop to look at things in the schoolyard. The younger children bow their heads when Sister Benitia lets go of my hand. My shoes are scuffed from the playground.

The schoolchildren watch me on the way home. They are whispering as I cross the tracks and head down the ravine to toss stones in the creek. There's a hill where Auntie Pomerinski's garden stands. She grows grapes in summer. "Auntie?" I say. I pull out these thistles from the field. My side hurts from everything happening at once. I look at the school, the Sisters. I see the flag of Poland.

I should bury something, I think, my scapular, my silver dollar. Before I get home I should study geography, trying harder to learn about the old country. I should help her in the garden.

"Auntie," I say. My face is wet. It is hard to breathe. "Auntie, Auntie, *czekać*," I say. "Wait!" I know if I run harder . . .

In the garden, butterflies come to meet me, then fly on. They brush and flutter about my shoulders. Because of them I can't see. Then they open a beautiful, long tunnel for me, and I feel their wings as I run through. At the end, behind Auntie's purple flowers, I know there's an empty chair in the house and that her dream book is open on the table. Crying, I run right through the butterflies now, all of them, all of the mourning cloaks, the blue and yellow ones, but they stay right with me and come into the house where the old Polish ladies are already washing her.

Children of Strangers

RALPH and Josie Slipkow-
ski live on Raspberry Avenue in a two-bedroom
bungalow which is not raspberry-colored but green with white
trim. They have a brass doorknob and an American eagle door
knocker which no one uses. Next to the door in summer a
planter full of petunias cheers things up. A beautiful sugar
maple also grows in their yard in Superior, Wisconsin, a railroad and port city whose motto, "Superior—Where Sail Meets
Rail," was coined during a Chamber of Commerce meeting at
the Androy Hotel on Tower Avenue. Ralph Slipkowski trims

and waters his lawn. With knife and spade, he edges a border along the sidewalk so no weeds can grow there. When Josephine needs emotional support, especially when she starts doubting again, he's around. Most people wouldn't believe anyone living in a well-kept house, whose appearance its owners take pride in preserving, would be uncertain in life. Houses like the Slipkowskis' should project their owners' stability and be signatures of the well-kept existence—and Josie and Ralph's is a modern, two-bedroom bungalow.

When Josie and Ralph examine themselves in the living room mirror, they see two people in decline. Ralph's been spending a lot of time in rooms with mirrors. This night Josephine arranges her hair, her husband his tie. Actually only Josie understands what's occurring around her. She sees no very good future for herself. Something's causing her to doubt. She thinks of herself as being on the verge of time, though never speaks of it this way. Poor Ralph doesn't see what's going on, Josie thinks. He's missing what stands right here before him in the mirror or outside on the street. Ralph has been kind and thoughtful. So have the kids. But he doesn't see what's going on, she thinks. He has nothing to fear; he can't read the signs in the mirror.

"You can tell really good, expensive mirrors by placing a fingertip to the glass," he says. "There'll be an eighth-inch, maybe more, reflected from where your fingertip touches to where the reflected one begins. Cheap mirrors don't reflect as deep as expensive ones. Expensive mirrors express a person better."

The oak dresser with Ralph and Josie's most expensive mirror stands in a house on an elm-lined street of houses which were kept up once, but now grow shabby. They aren't looked after. When they aren't painted, when little things go wrong, houses deteriorate. They've gotten so because people in Superior are out of work. The cold, rainy, foggy weather in summer only makes matters worse for the people and their houses, but not Ralph Slipkowski's house, for even in retirement, he's a tireless, meticulous worker, especially in a room with mirrors. The mirror on the oak dresser stands like a heart at the center of his house.

The nuns reside two miles from Ralph and Josie's. *Szkoła Wojciecha* means "Albert, or Adalbert School." The pupils have names like Maretski, Mizinski, Symczyk, Lalko, and Urbaniak. In school they are more sober and industrious than their parents were. Stanislaus Wysinski, the Slipkowskis' neighbor, has taken his boy to the window, pointed to section hands laying track on the Great Northern, and said, "You straighten out in school or you'll be hiding sand under the ties when you're old." Josef Stasiak, in an effort to get his grandson back in school, told the boy, who'd quit to work on the coal docks, "*Chciałeś, teraz masz.* You wanted it, now you have it." Ralph Slipkowski was like that with his sons. Ralph's life, Josie will tell you, hasn't been easy. He's wished for better, maybe a promotion to millwright. He's wanted the best for his boys. But there for a time when they wouldn't study, he'd had to lay down the law. "This is *my* mill. You'll do as I say."

"So, Ralph," Josephine says, "if life isn't easy for the nuns at least they have a job. Think of the years they've been here."

Ralph comes into the living room. "Is this tie on straight?" he asks as Josie, in an effort to forestall her decline, primps before the mirror.

"Those neighborhood kids drive the nuns crazy . . . Yes, it is, Ralph, the tie's straight. Right back to the Motherhouse, one right after another the nuns go. Lately it's worse."

Ralph rubs Butch Wax in his hair. After twenty-eight years, he still uses it. He still goes to Mass after twenty-eight years of marriage too, but irregularly. Ralph and Josie had talked and talked before he let the boys attend St. Adalbert's School.

"It's my duty to give them a Catholic education," Josie had argued.

"Public schools are fine," Ralph had said, "but if your heart's set."

The boys are out of school now and gone, and the old-timers leaving, thinks Josie. *Their houses fall apart.* She thinks of how the city moves indigent families into vacant houses near the Slipkowskis' when public housing near the Fraser Shipyards is full. It's nothing intentional, she knows, nothing against Ralph and her, but at the moment most of the vacant houses are near theirs. Some of the Polish people have died, others gone away. The city purchases their houses for below market value, and in rush the newcomers. Now the children of strangers break glass on the sidewalks, roar down the alleys on motorcycles, and let their dogs loose in the streets. These people who put up grease racks in the yard, Josephine has often wondered, where do they come from—out near Iron River or Brule? Her husband thinks nothing of it. He doesn't worry too much about other people. He glances once more in the mirror, glances fearlessly at himself in the expensive mirror on his grandmother's dresser.

Josephine straightens her collar, sprays a reluctant curl with VO5. Ralph Slipkowski still putters around the room. *The boys are gone,* Josie thinks, *I'm getting older.* Was it so easy raising two children, keeping house, and staying out of debt when the mill was down or Ralph sick? she wonders. She recalls the struggle, like the time Ralph went to work for someone else and found he couldn't make it and had to return to the mill.

For the past few months, even a year now, the Sisters have been on Josie's mind the way mirrors have been on Ralph's. The nuns live in the neighborhood with newcomers who can't get into shipyard housing. Sister Stella, Sister Cecilia, and Sister Appolonia have come and gone. Their coifs were made of hard, white, starched cloth, wimples thrust from their neck. Their lacquered beads swung as they walked. Sister Bronislaw has three new nuns to keep her company. The good sisters of *Szkoła Wojciecha* care for Father Nowak's vestments, order votive candles, sweep the sacristy, lead the choir, teach, and pray. Before lunch they pray several times.

Despite this, they are declining. Even the schoolchildren observe this. The children's own parents are losing the language. The neighborhood is failing. In the year the cornerstone was set, 1917, and after, students were more aware of their heritage, Josie thinks. Sister Bronislaw they learned to fear and admire. The trainer of wayward Polish youth instructed them—she trained us, me, thinks Josie—to work, to honor the Polish flag, to grow up in the faith. Now the neighborhood's gone to hell with people of different faith, or of no faith. "People without a heritage who draw public assistance have overtaken us, Ralph," she says to her husband.

He's looking in the bedroom mirror. Fearing nothing, he moves from mirror to mirror, room to room, good mirrors, bad mirrors. In the expensive mirror on his grandmother's dresser, the one in the bedroom, he can see himself reflected better. In fact, it's such a good mirror that he can almost see the past in it. His own past has never troubled him much.

"Ralph Slipkowski!" she calls.

He appears with a flourish. "Yes, I'm ready," he says. His hair is gray. It stands up with Butch Wax. The gray matches his tweed jacket. "It begins at 7:30, doesn't it?" he asks. His face beams with goodwill. "Let's say goodbye to the old girl." He jiggles the car keys. He helps Josephine with her coat. It is early winter in Josie Slipkowski's soul. What's coming will be worse, she thinks. She doubts she can survive. Extinction might be better, she tells herself.

"We've done OK, Ralph, haven't we?"

In the car she thinks of Sister Bronislaw. For a moment she doesn't know who she's talking to, like the good Sister is there with them.

"How quickly time flies," Josie says.

She hears Ralph's chuckle.

"What?" he asks.

"I was dreaming of Sister. Are you listening, Ralph? It's OK if you don't."

I understand you, Ralph, my dear. Content with himself, he drives on. *You've done much good for the nuns and Father, Josie thinks. Our sons are grown and gone away. And if you don't listen to me all the time now what does it matter? For twenty-eight years you've listened carefully. It's just that I don't know what our future holds. We're losing. I'm certain the strength of our family, our generation, is slipping away. Our boys, Warren and Terry, won't have the strength the Sisters brought with them from the old country. We are in decline, Ralph Slipkowski, and I am afraid.*

Ralph checks the rear view mirror. He signals, turns up East 5th Street. He goes by the East End library, Peters' Grocery.

You're a harmless, good man whose shortcomings are modest ones. You, Warren, and Terry never shared the old customs with me. Sometimes I fear for myself. It was an odd, holy house I grew up in. Blessed candles were stuck away in drawers and Holy Water in different rooms. Black crepe on the door signaled death. If we dropped bread, Grandma made us kiss it. History haunts me. You and the boys don't know how bad. Now we must look over our shoulders and lock our doors when we leave the house.

Humming, Ralph drives effortlessly. He passes the Northern Block. He turns one block down at the intersection by the drugstore and the bank.

Looking out the window, Josephine sees Mrs. Pawlokowski and Mrs. Fronckiewicz walking arm in arm. They are going the way of the Slipkowskis'. They wave. Ralph pulls onto 4th Street.

"Those old ones . . . ," he says.

But Josephine does not dismiss them easily, for on winter mornings, these same old ones, Mrs. Cieslicki, Mrs. Kiszewski, are here worshiping in the church of Polish immigrants. They come to Mass every day. In bitter weather the Sisters and the elderly pray as though it were summer. Nothing keeps them away. Why do old, weary legs come here, weary spirits arise to walk to a cold church where sometimes visiting priests say Mass? Over the years Josie Slipkowski has justified her own faith through the faith of others. She has realized that out of all the old ones, including her own grandmother, out of all the immigrants from Poznań and Szczecin, Warsaw and Białystok, at least one of them had more than simple ignorant faith to come each morning in prayer. One of them must have known something. This person—a peasant from Lodz, a baker from Katowice, a coachman from Zielona Góra—must have had a reason to think that getting up to pray was to be worth it. What the old ones have is faith that has traveled far, thinks Josie.

Szkoła Wojciecha stands at 3rd Street and 22nd Avenue. From there you can see Fredericka Flour, where Ralph Slipkowski worked all his days, the oil dock, Hog Island, the Left-Handed River. Father rings the bell. Ralph pulls up before Mrs. Konchak's garage. She waves her red kerchief. "It's OK," she says. *To dobrze.*

Downstairs you can smell coffee and flowers, cigarette smoke and baked goods. You can hear the roar of parish voices punctuated by laughter and song. Mr. Adam Burbul, Mrs. Tomaszeski, Augie and Louie Fronckiewicz and their mother and sisters, good, patient Helen Stromko from the dime store, the Nicoskis, Mrs. Cieslicki, Mrs. Podgorak—they have all assembled this Thursday evening. How Josephine Slipkowski wishes Warren and Terry, who went here eight years and played basketball in this hall, could see it, and her grandmother and grandfather, *Babusia* and *Dziaduś,* who are dead.

A classmate from 1934, a red-and-white carnation in his lapel, stands by the door. Ralph finds Josephine a chair. Father Nowak appears soon after the church bell has stopped. On stage sits Sister Bronislaw. The parishioners sing, *"Jeszcze Polska Nie Zginęła."*

How we're losing, thinks Josephine Slipkowski. *Except for their years at Szkoła Wojciecha, what will distinguish the young who change their names and move away? Beyond St. Adalbert's, what remains? Beyond the nuns . . . ?*

Josephine recalls her mother telling her how, in the old times, Sister Bronislaw went door to door to houses under quarantine. A purple card placed on the door by the Health Department meant typhoid, a red card, scarlet fever. Sister Bronislaw would inquire, "Do you need food, Mrs. Pomerinski? Forest wood?" She was never weak, Josie thinks.

The gym's beige and green paint has faded and chipped; the hardwood floor is warped. Steam pipes run along the walls. The Rosary Society has decorated them with red and white bunting. All the old parishioners are here.

"The old Polish people won't be with us much longer," Josephine says to Ralph. Sister herself has been here a half-century, thinks Josie. "Maybe not a week or a month, Ralph, and we'll read in the news that all of them have finally gone away."

Some of the old ones speak no English. Those who do sing "Joining Poland's Sons and Daughters, We'll be Poles Forever" before Father clears his throat. Except for his voice, the hall is quiet.

"Tonight is an honor," he says. "We're here to give you this tribute, Sister Bronislaw."

Settling her hands on her lap, Sister leans forward. She gazes at Father Nowak and down at the parishioners in the gym. She holds their gift, a little unsteadily—a red box with a white bow around it. Is it a scapular . . . a book of the lives of the saints wrapped in the colors of Poland? Josie wonders. Sister Bronislaw clasps it to her as she looks out at the walls she has known so long and at the people: a priest, a former novitiate, a grocer, and a newsman, a teacher and a banker and a Great Northern switchman, a worker in the drugstore, a street cleaner. Sister clutches the gift to the crucifix hanging from a gold chain around her neck. The parishioners' love goes with her.

"This," she says, "what's this?"

They stand to applaud.

Father Nowak reads a letter of good wishes. As others praise Sister Bronislaw, Sister Benitia plays "God, Who Held Poland" on the piano. The old hall rings with haunted melodies that hurt a person with their sadness, the unforgotten music of the past. How can you describe the music? Chopin . . . Paderewski . . . It is something romantic. . . .

The outsiders arrive the way they've been for centuries. Just as Sister and the others sing *"Jeszcze Polska"* they hear the slow, airy settling of the door. Having seen lights, no doubt the newcomers figured on shooting baskets in the gymnasium. The old people, as they prepare to be invaded, hear them chattering, snapping their gum, bouncing the ball. Except for an occasional cough and some scraping of chairs the hall is quiet. Even Father Nowak with the Bishop's letter tucked away in his jacket and Sister Bronislaw in her chair on the stage turn to the entrance at the bottom of the stairs, anticipating the noise, the violent entry into their lives.

The two boys, defiant in torn jackets, walk in as though they have every right to. The children of strangers, they have invaded the neighborhood. They come and go freely. As the young ones roam the alleys, their older brothers accost the meek and humble.

When they see the old Polish people the two boys stop. Hunched over, chewing their gum, they stare at the face of Poland, whose age and civility mean nothing to them. One boy is pasty looking. Dark circles ring his eyes. The other, having tried growing a moustache, has succeeded in raising a few stringy hairs on the upper lip. The two boys, not over thirteen or fourteen, waver there. They do not attend this school. Perhaps they've never been in its gym. Or perhaps, having found Mr. and Mrs. Novozinski, Albert Roubel, the Stefankos, and one hundred others, the boys have discovered Mrs. Josephine Slipkowski's "verge of time" and can't break free again to darkness and the night yet. In finding the old people they have found the past. It catches their imagination.

On the western front in 1939, Polish horse soldiers, their drawn swords raised and gleaming, charged German armored tanks. Defiantly, quixotically, soldiers from another century charged into the mechanical age and disappeared in the smoke. At the same time in Poland, young airmen practiced maneuvers in glider planes—not motorized airplanes like the enemy had, but glider planes. When Poland was finally lost to the enemy, the Polish State Radio broadcast a Polonaise and fell silent. The radio went off the air with something for dreamers.

Now in the gymnasium of the Polish school it is as if, through some stroke of fate, two intruders have discovered a forest clearing from which to observe horse soldiers gearing for the last, violent, fatal charge. In their one brief moment, the two witness for the first time their neighbors' nobility. It is evident in how the old people have turned out to honor the nun, in how they've kept up their traditions, their faith. While it has taken Josephine some months of constant doubting to observe, then to accept the newcomers' disregard for others, these children of strangers have taken only a minute to learn about centuries of struggle and grow bored. Wearying of the moment, the boys no longer appear to care what has been discovered this night. You could give them Sobieski charging the Turks, thinks Josie, Dąbrowski praying in his tent for a safe return from Italy, the Black Madonna pierced in the side and crying, Unrug at the Battle of Hel. You could give them Thaddeus Kosciuszko freeing Warsaw from the Russians in the Spring of 1794, and the two intruders wouldn't care. These things resonate in the air about them. They lie in the mirrors in the Polish homes and in the wrinkles of the old faces and in the eyes and deep within the memory.

"What they staring at us for?" the boy with the circles under his eyes says. They bounce the ball, spy the table with the food and cake for Sister Bronislaw. The other intruder spits out his gum, puts up a shot. The basketball, falling through, rips the paper decorations hanging from the net. It is a long, hopeless, ugly moment as they saunter to the table laden with sweetbreads, hot dishes, hams, cheese, pickles, the large white cake.

"I'm not standing in line," the boy with the moustache says.

"Why should we?" the other says. Tossing the ball against the wall, he catches it, hands it to his partner, who throws it up again.

"They'll be gone," Josie whispers to Ralph. "Then there'll be a Polonaise."

But Ralph is not looking on the bright side. The intruders walk past Stel Nowatski, Mr. Mrozynski, Mr. Mackiewicz, Mrs. Kosmatka. When they pass him, the smirking boys do not look at Ralph, but *through* him as though he counts for nothing at all on this earth. That's when he has a vision of the days to come. Looking at the other parishioners' faces, for a moment he can't see his own reflected, not in their glasses, not in their eyes, not in their Polish words. Suddenly nothing reflects Ralph Slipkowski of Superior, Wisconsin. It's not his wife's but his thinking about the future that changes now. More and more in the coming days, he sees in this vision of a world without depth, riots will be tearing cities apart, and presidents and dignitaries will be seized and put upon. It is not Josie's but Ralph Slipkowski's thinking that's changed. And now, of all things, he's suddenly becoming frightened of looking ahead.

Tango of the Bearers

of the Dead

WHAT did he see that he'd come so often to my house and cup my face in his hands? What was this man looking for who was not my husband?

At the top of the mirror a plain wooden border forms a scroll with lilies carved around it. As a child I was left to imagine the devil. Below the scroll is my hair, which I have pulled in a knot. It has kept some of its color. Though I am hardly younger than my husband, my skin has stayed soft. My mouth curves down at the corners. When I hold my neck this way or that the skin stretches under my chin. No matter how I try to dust and polish them away I see the imperfections of my face, so I discourage remembering. I am not grateful to God for my years. The mirror on the dresser is too honest with me.

I've imagined the devil, wondered at his looks. Once in *Biały Brzeg* before we came here, my father told me a story. "There was a girl who would not help her mother," he said. "The girl would lie around the cottage. She'd stain her lips with berries, then rise to wash the berry stain from her lips and look in the mirror. Her father and the priest warned her, but she couldn't get enough of her beauty, the desirable eyes, the raspberries that stained her lips and cheeks. Her old grandmother lived there. When the old woman got sick the girl wouldn't help. She gave her time to the mirror—until one day she saw the devil. She threw the mirror down, cried out, pulled her hair. Each time she looked . . . the devil. Early in the morning or at midnight in the firelight's glow, she saw herself and her new companion. She had spent so much time gazing at herself that she was being repaid. The devil never went away. He was there whenever she looked. The devil's lips were as red with berry juice as her own."

"*Djabeł*, demons!" I say and put down the cloth I polish with.

On my knees I pray to the cross. I beg to be forgiven, to have it as though I was never here and all things about me are forgotten. I see Him reflected in the mirror, the whole room reflected; its chairs, the clock that sounds the hour four as I kneel, the painting of Jesus on the wall above the crucifix. "*O jakie to szczęście moje,*" I pray to Him.

My husband lies in a bed.

"How is he?" I inquire of my grandson.

"I'm afraid not good, *Babusia*. Lorraine and Bernice are there. My mother too."

"He's old. He couldn't go on long," I say to Vincent, who listens intently.

My grandson takes a chair, studies my vase and the oil lamp which has been converted to use electricity. I do not turn it on. Without the rose lamp's glow there is less to remember. The room has an odd, shadowy peace similar to my garden at sunset. A moment before, I had prayed to be forgotten. The peonies my husband hand-painted on the lamp's globe grow a delicate green toward the top. The apple tree bough rubs the window by the mirror where I'd been studying my face and how best it could be forgotten. "He wanted the whole tree cut down," I say. "Do you want me to wind his watch?"

"Let me," my grandson says, taking the key.

Listening to me, watching me recall my life, Vincent must see my age, my eighty-four ungrateful years. At Christmas we sing *Wśród Nocnej Ciszy* or *Bóg Się Rodzi* and break *opłatki* with each other. At Easter I prepare the food for nieces and nephews and have an egg hunt for the grandchildren. In summer I work in the garden. I want him to see how thin I've become, that I have a hard time hearing, and that listening is a burden. My grandson must see I am as frail as the past, not worth visiting. I want no visitors, yet he is a troublesome one. This boy who is already in his middle thirties and has my daughter's blood, this grandson says to me that everywhere he feels the loss of the past. Why should he bother with the past?

My husband's beautiful watch is meant for the vest or trousers pocket; the chain and the key to be kept in another pocket or hung across the vest front. My dying father gave the watch to Antoni in the old country. Was it to be a wedding present? My husband Antoni is dying. We were the children of strangers.

"Grandmother, I must tell you it's difficult for me to come here," my grandson Vincent says. "Grandpa Tony weighs on me. I haven't any memories of him."

Too late the words escape my lips. "Look at his watch!" I say.

The thin hands point the hours. Between the XII and VI stands a small hand to tell seconds, below that the Russian writing. He sees the tiny figures carved delicately in the silver—the horse's mane, the slight upward curve of the sled's runner blades, the driver's scarf in the wind. He thinks it's a Russian watch. Turning the watch over in his hand, Vincent sees Georges FAVRE Jacat, Locle, ARGENT written in a larger hand.

"The Russians have no ability to make a watch. The face of a watch, the key, the chain, the vest pocket to put it in perhaps, but no inner workings," I say. "They are Swiss."

"I know about my father's side of the family, Grandmother. It's this side that eludes me. I know less about it."

An airplane interrupts our stillness. It crosses for just a second between the sky and the house, casting its shadow on the table. Vincent knows so little about his grandfather because Antoni and I never spoke of the past. For fifty years one thing separated us. We ate together and raised children together, but remained apart.

"Before your great-grandfather died he gave the watch to me. It was for my husband, your grandfather, whose dying now bothers you," I say. "Once my husband asked to see the watch. I said I'd show him another time. He knew right off I didn't have it." (I think to myself how Frank Kornacki, who was not my husband, had been gambling and drinking in the town those days. He came here and cupped my face in his hands.) "Why did my husband worry about a watch?" I ask my grandson. "When he had time off from work he'd go downtown on the trolley, 'Do you have my watch? Was my wife here with it?' he'd ask in stores. One day at the closest store to home that Antoni could look into, the jeweler Yano sold it back to him. It wasn't Yano's fault. He didn't know its value when he bought it."

My grandson traces the shadow of the apple tree on the table. "What a bitter story. You didn't pawn it, did you?"

We sit quietly, the watch and chain in my hands.

"Can you bring out grandfather's violin?" he asks.

He is persistent. He asks me about things I wish to forget. I've watched over him since the cradle. Does he drink? I wonder. How sensitive is he to his wife? Wrinkles on his face remind me of my own face.

"I used to hear Polish soldiers singing," I tell him. "They had no reason to be happy. Now my husband is dying. I was with him this morning in the hospital, but Bernice took me home to rest. I always remember the 'Tango of the Bearers of the Dead' they sang."

"Because you think we're bearers of something?"

"Maybe our memories . . . for those who want them. Let's talk about him then, Vincent. Let's say he's here now. Your grandfather, my husband, came with the new century. We were born in *Biały Brzeg,* 'White Shores.' There were forests, rivers. He was a quartermaster in the Russian Army. Have you seen his photograph, Vincent? His Russian uniform has a tunic collar with two scarlet squares. They could tint photographs. Your grandfather, who is dying, went home on furlough, didn't return to their army. I knew him in *Biały Brzeg.* I was already in America. I don't know whether he told anyone he was leaving. Like most Poles, he was coming to America to strike it rich. He hated the Russians. I made him no promises. He played this violin. He dressed as a musician traveling about to fairs and weddings on the border. He had to pay to cross. He had to have money for the train to the sea and for passage over. This part of town was almost all Polish people when he got here. Time has shrouded things, and I can't explain some of them.

"It's like a knot," I tell my grandson. "How do you untie it? Your grandfather built the house. He went to the ironworks

and chair factory where he lost three fingers one day. He culti-
vated the garden. My husband could do a *Kozak* dance the
way you . . . what do you do now?" *I've seen too much. I
can't look in the mirror without memory,* I think.

The floral print dress is thin on my arms and back. I put on
the sweater. "I'm chilled," I say. I take the violin and motion
to my grandson who comes with me down the steps to the
back yard whose grass needs cutting. The sun feels good after
the house. I lay the violin against the chair. The rich blue
clematis has opened out. I retie the knot of twine which holds
the vine to the trellis.

"Grandmother Mizinska, come sit down here. We have a
pocket watch and a violin."

We sit in chairs in a garden which over the years has become
a place of memories I wish to forget. In order to destroy them,
I will treat the garden with salt, plant it deep. Vincent has
spent much time here with me. I lay the violin on my lap. In
places its wood is scratched. For years I have cut back raspberry bushes, wishing they were memories. Dreams hang like
fragile glass in the air of the garden. They grow out of the fertile earth. Hidden in the twisting grapevines whose leaves obscure the rotting garden posts, hidden in the cool, moist earth
turned up by my spade, hidden in shadows of the corn rows,
the dreams and memories intoxicate my grandson and make
him a lover of the past.

Frank Kornacki was here. He worked in a hotel, I think to
myself. *He laid his heavy hands on my shoulders once when Antoni was bringing in wood. My father couldn't stand this hosteler
Kornacki from Warszawa. I was married. He came again to this
house when Antoni was gone to work. Frank Kornacki pulled me
to the floor. Though I was pregnant, he was a gambler.*

"*How much do you love me, Róża Mizinska?*" *Frank Kornacki would ask.*

"Very much," I'd say.

"How much?"

He traced the outline of my forehead with hands that held a deck of playing cards all night long. As the clock struck the hour, I would trace the outline of his cheek with my lips.

"How much, Róża?"

"Enough to sell my husband's watch."

When he left I would put the crucifix on the wall, pray awhile, then prepare Antoni's supper. I'd hum and sing as I did my house chores. I'd sinned, yet managed to look in the mirror on the dresser to run my delicate fingers over the places Frank Kornacki had been. This went on several months when Antoni was away at work.

Antoni and Frank Kornacki one Sunday gambled and drank in the tavern. Frank Kornacki was losing. Frank Kornacki said, "Give me the eight dollars, Mizinski, and I'll tell you something about your wife!"

"Your grandfather Antoni planted a border of flowers here," I tell my grandson. "Bachelor buttons, petunias, pink and white phlox . . . see how abundantly they grow . . . yellow, scarlet, purple flowers in whose midst you can dance. During dry spells Antoni watered the garden with rain water from the barrel . . . I think with his tears, too, for coming to America."

"I feel grandfather here, don't you, *Babusia?*" he says.

"It's due to the stories which have been told here and the songs played on a concertina and a violin."

I lower my voice, try to forget. Vines, stems, leaves speak as the wind shifts. Like all the other times, the will to remember returns, too strong yet to be abandoned.

I tell Vincent how his Grandfather Antoni Mizinski placed lighted candles on his own grandmother and grandfather's grave in Poland. "In the darkening fields at summer's end, the goldenrod and caraway brushed his legs, Vincent. From the brittle caraway he pulled the seeds. In the mountain ash trees robins ate the red berries, and he always thought the fermenting berries eased the pain of leaving."

"*What will I do for my pain in America?*" *my husband asked me after Frank Kornacki was here.* "He forced you down with his hand to your throat, didn't he?"

"*Yes, Antoni Mizinski.*"

"*Then I will have him arrested.*"

"*But our good name! What will our good name suffer?*"

Antoni Mizinski, the tears in his eyes, grabbed me, shook me so I feared for the baby . . .

I hear the airplane, notice the breeze from the lake and the bay of Superior. He is dying.

"*Przebóg,* bless me," I say.

On his bedstand in the hospital is the prayer book he's had since childhood. The holy card inside says, "If we can contemplate the mutual love of Jesus and His Mother, how can we fail to be partners of Their Joys?"

"He worked in the ironworks and in the chair factory," I say. "He built ninety-two pew boxes for the church. He had three children, farmed many years, had a smile for me, Vincent, but what he must have experienced coming over from the old country," *and what he must have thought of me. He held it in. It's true I believe in night terrors and wolves and demons. Where do things go when they're no longer remembered? Do they go far into the depths of some mirrors?* "Frank Kornacki—"

"What, Grandma?" my grandson says.

"In the old country we were closer to the days when things might inhabit a mirror, Vincent. My curious grandson, I want you to forget about all of us who've gone before you. I want you to forget me and all the things that embarrass a family and make it small. Bear your dead some other way. I am done remembering."

Frank Kornacki . . . I sold the watch, and he took the money for gambling and tobacco, three-eighths of a pound of machorka a week. I said to him, "Don't smoke. I fear Antoni will smell it in here." Frank Kornacki kept at it. He smiled. "I'm a gambler," he said and showed me his playing cards.

"Will you take me to the hospital, Vincent, so I may see my husband?" I ask the grandson. The sky has turned purple. He helps me with my chair and holds my arm up the stairs to the kitchen porch. The watch and violin I place on the mantelpiece. Even for this late in summer the wind is cold out of the northern sky.

We pass the abandoned chair factory, the abandoned store where Antoni Mizinski recovered the watch. The dying fields stretch out forever to the bay. They were so flat you could see Frank Kornacki's horse two or three miles away grazing in the yard behind his house. There was room in this town to walk and hide in. No one knew but Antoni.

My husband's face is familiar to me, nothing more. His head lies on a pillow. If memory couldn't interfere, part of me would be dying. But I remember a gambler. *He was different, Antoni. I knew he'd die before us.*

My husband looks as he did yesterday and the day before. Bernice and Lorraine have stepped out to talk about things. My oldest daughter Gertrude weeps in the hall. No change has occurred but the slight bruise on the hand which would have held the bow when he played at harvest weddings. He is dying, Antoni Mizinski is dying.

Vincent whispers to him. He is the inquisitive one wanting

to remember. I have no use for the past. One of my daughters must have combed Antoni's white hair and wiped his lips. Another old man lies moaning in the bed by the window. Is he as old?

"Grandpa Tony," Vincent says.

Something holds your attention, my husband. You are busy. You thrash and grow still. What are you concentrating on that your eyes stare large at the corner of the room? For what reason have you pursed your mouth? Your arms are tied with cloth at the wrist and cloth ties you to the bed. The sheets are rumpled. "Let me fix them," I say. *You are safe. Without memories or shadows you have nothing to fear.*

"It is your wife, Róża Mizinska," I whisper.

You stop your wandering to look up, as though you have heard unwelcome news not worth eight dollars. Your fingers work against the knot. Is it the knot of forgiveness? What lies in undoing it, Antoni? No matter how it eludes you, you keep on, my husband of fifty years. I would like to know, does anything matter to you that you persevere, Antoni? You lived, played the violin, raised up our three children, who now make arrangements for you outside the door. Nothing matters to Róża Mizinska, you know.

I say to Vincent, "Eighty years ago he came here with his violin. Over the roads, smiling and waving. Oh, Lord! He told me he prayed and hid from soldiers. In places rain and wind beat down the grass for him. He would lie unobserved and listen to the wind. To see where he'd be in his journey, he'd brush aside the goldenrod to look for the telegraph poles, the orchards, the paths he'd see tomorrow." *I was already here with Frank Kornacki fumbling the laces of my blouse. But I made no promise. In some places with the wolves crying, how you must have feared the night, Antoni. I was waiting. Things took care of themselves except that you learned too*

much for your money. Now there is a knot left you try to under-
stand. The hospital is filled with old ones trying to undo their
knots. Let me untie it. Let me undo these laces for you, Frank
Kornacki. I want you to feel the child in my belly.
  "How much do you love me, Róża Mizinska?"

Vincent kisses your hand. "Goodbye, Antoni," he says.

It is late. I leave my daughters. Some of our grandchildren
have arrived in the hall. I begin thinking of the dead. Vincent
drives me home. The priests have told us all along that the
dead would rise. It is bleak in the fields with the sun going
down. I hope you are all right, my husband. "Rest," they
told me.

I read the Polish newspaper. I have a quiet supper. After-
ward I sit alone in my chair in my part of the house. The phone
rings when I don't expect it. "It's about father," Lorraine says.
I feel the weather change.

I go to bed on the night of your death, Antoni. You are
gone now. What point in staying up? As I pray for you, the
strangest thoughts trouble me. I am an old woman. The world
has changed. We started our journey way in the past. You told
me you prayed while strange sounds haunted the woods. It
was sometime long after planting and sowing, and when the
caraway was all around you in the fields. You, a journeying
man, having prayed to Almighty God, sat and played your violin without fear. Tell me, when you praised God and uttered
your hopes for me in America, was it worth it? Tell me . . .

I read your obituary the same morning I bring up the black
paint from the basement.

Born in 1880, Antoni Mizinski was a city resident employed for many years by the Webster Chair Factory
and the Marine Ironworks. Later he farmed in the area.

A member of St. Adalbert Church and the Thaddeus Kosciuszko Fraternal Lodge, he is survived by his wife, three daughters, eight grandchildren, thirty great-grandchildren, two great-great-grandchildren. . . .

"Goodbye, Antoni," I say. It is mid-September when I throw the last flowers and dirt on your grave.

I try to get my dreams to go away, but they are with me each night as is common in the season of remembering: until one morning now in the dead of winter when terrible storms threaten the north, I rise and walk down the cold stairs to the mirror in the living room. The chairs are in place. The clock sounds the hour. I know where we acquired each item in this room, the doilies on the chair arms, the vase of lilacs and peonies in the spring, the wooden crucifix over the mantel, the painting of the Christ child above that, your prayer book *ANIÓŁ STRÓŻ*, Antoni.

Christ and the devil meet in a mirror. Here you see either His perfect world reflected, or deception, disillusionment, despair. Not having slept so well these past few months, my face is drawn. I will look like this in the coffin. I wear the things of the past: at my throat, the brooch of Grandmother Catherine Wilenski; around my wrist, a cheap bracelet of Frank Kornacki, a gambler and violator of everything; on my finger, the ring from you, my dear husband. In a month or a year I will look like what I see in the mirror this last time, Antoni, an old, ruined woman whose hair and eyes I never wish to see again . . . whose lips and throat . . . whose breasts and shoulders I take away from her . . . whose arms, whose old, old body I take away. As I lift the paintbrush over and over the glass of the living room mirror, paint drips patterns on the floor. There is no more remembering God's perfect work. I have no face, no body remains, nothing remains after I paint its reflection . . . this room, this violin, this Russian watch, this picture of Christ. No lamp is here reflected, no table.

Afterwards, after the memory of grandmothers and grandfathers, aunts and uncles, Fryderyk in the old country, Brygida, Elżbieta, Jadwiga is gone, I clean the brush of its paint.

When my grandson visits in the morning, when he ambles through the wind, delighting in the pure driven snow from the north, no one will be found at home. All memories will have vanished, all time have stopped.

Durum Wheat

SIX or seven years after the last one left, another comes in. Andy Borzynski, who was sweeping flour dust around the mill, drops his broom, makes the Sign of the Cross, and runs into the boiler room. He tries telling who's come.

"What's got into you?" we ask, putting down our sandwiches.

When he's excited his hands fly around. Those are his languages and his prayers.

We don't like what walks in behind him, an Indian with his hair braided. They've got it good on the reservation with Bingo, then they start agitating for other rights.

"Jeezus," Roy Jorgenson says. "It's the kid of the old man."

"Who?"

"It's OK," Roy says. "It's Joe Bluebird's kid from a long, long time back."

Standing with his red and white cap, his two braids hanging down his shirt, and his turquoise belt on, the Indian looks like what we've been saying we hated in northern Wisconsin. Some of us guys have maybe never seen one recently. We knew if we did, it'd look like him.

"The Indian's been all over the world since he was last here as a kid," Roy says. "There's no place like home."

"How many Indians left, Roy?" asks one of the guys who moved to Superior a few years ago.

"Just some women on the waterfront who drive over from Duluth. Greek boats, Korean boats, Polack boats . . . it don't matter as long as the sailors got money. Your Dad worked here once, didn't he?" Ben Vermouth asks the Indian. "You still got an old auntie or something lives in the house?"

"Real old-timer," Bluebird says.

The Indian would look better without braids. His skin shines like it's been polished with a good, rich cloth.

"I told her we better move," the Indian, Gerald Bluebird, says about his wife.

"Move from where?"

"Just from all over around here."

Nobody, not one, said he was coming, I think. We have to be ready for the weekend shutdown we do every three months and to tape the doors and windows so the air can't get in or the poison, the methyl bromide, get out—and here we got a new one who doesn't know where he came from.

"Do you know how to handle a broom?" Ben Vermouth asks.

"You better tuck in that hairdo around the machines," Ed Van Holbeck says.

The Indian moves the braids over his shoulders so they hang down in back. They get him a locker, a push broom. "You've gotta get all around in here by the belts and pulleys," we tell him. "Sweep respectfully. See along the floor here? This flour dust is the excess of the milling process. It's still His Holy Body, though, you know."

"Whose body?" Gerald Bluebird asks.

"All this in here, the spring wheat and durum—," Eddie says.

By the end of the day we have him thinking we mill holy wafers for the churches. It's a hard-luck place, the town. If you take the "Su-" out of Superior, add the "-beria" from Siberia, you have "Suberiar," the place of rust and cold, the place of outcasts. There's rust for every saint in every church on every corner—and for those that don't believe, there's nondenominational rust. But worship it you must.

Andy Borzynski, the dummy, doesn't like when we joke about God or heaven. The dummy knows more than we ever give him credit for. One thing you don't mess with around him is God. So if we wait till Andy Borzynski goes to the packing floor before we start loud-talking about the mill, then it's not our fault if the Indian listens to our religious instructions to him.

"This is everything we say it is on the floor. We can't help that it falls, but we can sweep it up fast and reverently, which is where your broom comes in," Eddie says to him.

"Respectfully now, please," Roy and Benny say, "like it's God you're sweeping into little piles by the belts and pulleys where you pick it up in a dustpan. This was the dummy's job, but he's been promoted to prayer warden of the packing floor."

"See this bread we're eating?" Eddie says. "It's milled right here." He brushes the crumbs from his shirt.

At Fredericka we mill a first-rate product. The Fredericka manual reads, "To believe in the top-quality, the millhand has to get along with others." Indian or no, that is the God we worship—the manual and the togetherness of a top-quality product. We are men with a mission. No polished skin or hair braids will get in our way.

So the next day here is the Indian with his braids and his turquoise belt plus now he's carrying a thing that has a feather and beads which we figure he's going to toss into the boiler because he wants to be like the rest of us, but which he hangs up in plain sight on the front of his locker.

"It's a dream catcher," he says. "I couldn't get the flour dust out of my eyes last night."

"You should offer your soul up to Him," Benny says.

All this about the soul and the sacred dust of Fredericka's floors is a joke on an Indian—on our dummy too, who's never fully converted to the Fredericka way of thinking. Guys down here have played with the dummy's beliefs but it's never changed him a bit. To our way of thinking, he was baptized foreign. Our faith is in durum and spring wheat, in semolina milling. The shutdown that occurs is our Ash Wednesday. Every three months we close for the flour beetle and for other pests with polished shells that infest a mill. We post the doors, clear everyone out, and open up the methyl bromide into pipes that lead to all six floors. Nothing escapes the fumigating gas, which settles into places we cannot reach.

Now Andy Borzynski watches the Indian, trying to understand him. It's never been us Andy's listened to, never us who have done a lot for the dummy. He decided long back that we aren't worth listening to, for all we ever do is make fun of him.

"You should offer up your soul," Benny says to the Indian as Andy, the dummy, watches him.

"I did. I brought home flour last night. This morning," Bluebird says, "I could see dust rising from the windows of the mill when I came down. If you say it's God, then He is atop the waters of the bay, so it must work when I sweep."

He is right, too. Wheat-dust clouds hang over the mill. If you look at them long enough, it's like the Body of Christ.

"*Fader vår som är i himmeln,*" says Roy in Swede as if there's been a miracle.

All morning the Indian goes at it sweeping. Wind flutters in the dream catcher when Roy comes in from the coal yard. All morning the dream catcher, hanging on Bluebird's locker, catches drafts from the boilers.

"What is it exactly?" Van Holbeck asks at lunch.

We are all there when Bluebird says it's a little cut-off branch of red willow tied in a circle. "See the string that holds it? Over the inside of it, this stringy stuff is deer sinew. Hanging down from the circle are horsehairs, a goose feather."

Listening with his hands, the dummy is up next to Bluebird leaning on the locker, feeling the horsehairs. The Indian never tells us exactly what the dream catcher does, though. Andy Borzynski flings his hands up, makes the Sign of the Cross, then tries to pray or something but no words of spirit come out.

Every time we walk into the boiler room from that point on there's Andy, a deaf and dumb one, his fingers to the dream catcher.

"Andrzej . . . *na zdrowie,*" we say, which is what the Polacks who work here say when they drink. "Andy, get back to work!"

When Ted, the floor boss, needs to start taping for shutdown, we tell him Andy's all worked up. When it comes to poisoning time Ted gets excited. "Well, we've got to stay on schedule," he says. Coming back out of the boiler room, he says, "What's the thing on the Indian's locker?"

"It's his dream catcher," Benny says.

"What's that?"

"We don't know," Eddie says. "Some kind of circle."

"Get the Indian," Ted says.

When we find him on third floor, flour dust has gotten into his eyebrows. We try to keep the joke going, even though Ted's waiting downstairs for us to bring the Indian.

"You'll get the Fredericka spirit yet," Eddie says.

Bluebird has a hard time leaving the flour dust, like he's almost converted, like the spirit has got him. Flour has discolored him into being white. It's what this world is all about at the Fredericka Mill of Superior, Wisconsin.

We bring Bluebird downstairs to his locker. "Jeezus . . . ," Ted says about Andy, the dummy. "Look at him. He stares at that damn dream catcher like it's the risen Christ."

The dummy looks like he's choking on prayers he doesn't understand. With the flour on his face, it's difficult looking at him, at the strange, foreign face, at his hands on the dream catcher.

"Careful of your language around the dummy," Benny says.

"Jesus," Ted says to the Indian next. "Will you explain what this thing is doing here? If you want to be a Fredericka Flour man, you tell us what t'hell is hanging on your locker."

"A dream catcher. Good dreams float down the feather . . . see?" says Bluebird as Andy Borzynski touches it. "If you have this hanging up over your bed, you won't have bad dreams. Bad dreams catch among the webbing."

"So this thing hanging, that's *all* it is?" says Ted.

"Yeah," says Bluebird.

"Well you and him better get back to work. You two had better tape every place that opens up on the outside world," Ted says. "Mills are dangerous. You other boys get on now, too. We've got to have her up for fumigating. You and the dummy get taping. You others, get back to work. Your dreams are taken care of."

The feather and the red willow have satisfied the dummy like nothing else, it appears. He doesn't want to leave. Only when Ted shows him a picture of Jesus' patient heart does Andy get up.

All afternoon the dummy, Andy Borzynski, tapes along the edges of Fredericka's windows. From sixth to fourth he tapes. After an hour working in the boiler room, he tapes two more floors as Bluebird sticks up the POISON GAS signs. "Will you listen?" Bluebird keeps saying to the dummy.

This is one strange Indian, I think after watching him. He is not a key Fredericka player, bringing in a dream catcher as though he's pulling something on us. Benny and I observe him from behind the pulleys. Maybe Bluebird forgets because he mutters Indian things with no one around. God, those braids! It isn't us that're ugly. We aren't poisoned of spirit. We see how he's taped the signs crooked in the window, used too much tape.

At three o'clock, Benny, Ed, and Roy get up their cribbage game in the boiler room. Bluebird's saying things like "It's a good day to die." But nothing comes out of Andy Borzynski in response, nothing but his prayers, nothing except for once when there was something we partly missed, something said as Roy "pegged ten" on the cribbage board. "It's a good day to die" was only the last part of what this Indian said and the dummy responded to.

"What? What, Bluebird?" we ask, done joking. The methyl-fine mist will poison everything. Along the silent walls where we once stood to watch among places sealed for drafts, there has never been any doubt, any poison, I think. Now the unlikable Indian coming in here like this . . .

When the Indian punches his time card, looking up at the old place that employed his dad, he says Indian things concerning life and death and walks out, leaving the dream catcher on his locker. What does he mean, a good day? Nothing has died.

No one's been killed here unless he's talking about Andy, the dummy. Fredericka spirit is alive and well. We bet each other that the Indian didn't even sweep third floor right, but we can't go back up to check because it's poisoned now—everything is.

He walks out, and Jesus if it isn't snowing. April and the ground is white, and here is an Indian with white flour on his face like a white man walking a path through this stand of aspen where plastic bags and old newspapers catch in the trees.

Through the snow and early evening light I think I hear him praying. I don't know. It's hard to see with the swirling snow, but Bluebird is praying, it sounds like. And now the dummy runs after him, goes right out the mill door after him, flour on his face, hands talking like he's got something to say to him. "Hey wait!" we call. "You forgot your lunch pail." I don't know where the dummy goes . . . maybe away through the trees to the Left-Handed River. Maybe to follow the creek to its source in the wetlands. Maybe into the pine barrens as night hushes his footsteps. There's land to disappear in out there for an Indian true enough, voices from many years ago. Maybe by morning when the mist starts up, both will have found something in common. After a while Benny and I have to give up watching and go our separate ways home to supper.

Jalousie

I

I'VE trimmed my moustache so thin that to find it on my face I need a makeup mirror with magnified glass. Something Argentine was to have ridden above the lip, a pencil-thin moustache so black as to seize a woman's heart. But what do I see? A moustache like a decaying centipede. The razor has gouged my unstable lip so that I may cry. I comb my hair, put in my uppers. Even with these, my face appears sunken in the glass, and I think I may cry.

I reach for the black shoe polish, hum along. I know the words to Gardel's scratched recordings. "A Media Luz" describes the interior of an apartment where the table is always set for love. Another goes, "In my life I've had many many *minas*, but never a woman." I spear a toothpick into the shoe polish to trace in the missing moustache . . . darken my eyebrows. "I am nobody," I whisper. "It is the tango which triumphs."

Throwing off my robe, I see in nylon support hose, white underpants, and sleeveless T-shirt the romantic face, if not the body, of the great Valentino. I, Mr. Keeto, raise a waxy eyebrow to the mirror. Hand on hip, I whisper as though at a tea dance in the palm court of a Buenos Aires hotel, "You'll see love's nothing . . . the world doesn't give a damn."

"Good morning," I call to Mrs. Kovanic at the end of the hall. "Will you share this car with me, dearest?"

"Shut up, fruitcake!" she says, turning into her room.

"The bitterness and rage of not being," I whisper when no one gets on the elevator. "The failure of the dream that I sought to live," I say at seventh floor. "What for?" at sixth. Though unsure of its meaning, "*Soy el tango milongón,*" I sing to the fifth floor.

I know I will have to pass the Activities Room where the painting class meets. A good time to practice contrabody motion, I think.

Wearing a coat over the tango outfit, carrying hat and shoes in a shopping bag, I step out of the elevator with my left foot, bring my right shoulder slightly forward. All the way through the foyer I do a motion meant to enhance one's appearance in the dance. Left foot forward, right shoulder forward, I think, waving to the ladies.

"Where to, Joe?" Mrs. Laverdiere asks.

"Dance lessons, dearest," I say. Doing a series of rocking steps, a Reverse Copacabana, I do not regain my contrabody motion until the parking lot where their laughing stops.

Ah, *muchachos,* the city where I study, if you could see! It is dirty and rundown. No place has the proper "palm court" atmosphere. To such a neighborhood I, Mr. Keeto, a *compadrito* of the finest order, must drive my '49 Mercury limo with luggage racks on top. At safe speeds I make my way down the avenues.

The studio where I dance, *muchachos* (I am always relieved to arrive and to be out of traffic), stands in a spiritless neighborhood of taverns like The Bolero and the Whoop 'N Holler, run-down warehouses and, well, worse. Old men practice "Hesitation Steps" and "Biltmores." HERNANDO'S HIDEAWAY OPEN 2-NIGHT, the sign says.

Edward opens the door. He looks up and down the street to see that no one's followed me.

"Tango," I whisper.

I meet her in an upstairs parlor, my beloved Joyce.

"Lemme fix my face," she says. "You go on ahead . . . limber up. Say, Joe, something wrong with you?"

I purse my lips. "The tango is illusion," I say. "First, you feel with your head, then with your heart. You're a brush, Joyce, with which I shall draw my will upon the dance floor."

"No, here . . . for your lip. Here's a hankie."

When she walks out of the room I take up the posture in case she is watching.

"Lip? Lip?" I say. "What's wrong with my lip, she wants to know."

I hear her in the hallway talking to Eddie.

"Let's ease up. I'm not gonna clip the old guy anymore. He looks like a fool in that tango hat with the doodads hanging off the brim," Joyce says.

"Shut up. He'll hear."

"I don't care, Eddie. I don't care. He comes here with this black stuff on his lip. I'll be damned . . . looks like shoe polish."

Back at the apartment they call me the fool, the fruitcake, but here in my black high-heeled shoes of the type they wore in the *suburbios* of Buenos Aires one hundred years ago, here things are different. I, Joe Keeto, am agreeable to her.

Waiting for my Joyce I do the cha-cha-cha. With sambas in one parlor, foxtrots in another, I come to her, Señor Keeto of the black lips and tango shoes. I have lumbago and my hands shake, but when I am able, we work on slow, quick counts.

II

"Joe," she tells me when I am done with the Argentine Walk for the day, "you should keep up, you're so good."

"Please to call me José," I say. "Slow . . . slow . . . quick . . . quick," I count, then disappear with a dip and a glide.

Joyce catches me outside. "Joe," she says, lighting a cigarette. "At Hernando's this week I'm teaching the senior citizens a little mambo, a little cha-cha. I need some extra money. You know, the coffee fund."

"You can have money for tango instructions," I say. "But that's it . . . no more for a while."

Eddie helps me into the car, Joyce close behind. "*Muchas gracias,* José," she says as I pull away into the streets of Superior.

III

Nearing seventy years of age, I, the señor, do not listen at the apartments when they say I was never a *tanguero* but a maker of buns. My "corté," a dip step taken backward by the man, is so elegant and youthful that how could I have been a baker? Once I tried a corté on Mrs. Kovanic in front of the elevator in the apartment complex, but I misjudged the weight of the poor señora, and now she will not talk to me. Ah, but Joyce of Hernando's! She is another story. She is in love with tango-master Keeto.

Alone in my limo I hear the cursing, people gesturing as their cars pass. My centipede moustache quivers. My teeth are stained. Cars honk at me; now the tears. Yes, I *was* a baker. I know in my inmost heart I worked the wiener bun detail on the midnight shift at the Taystee Bakery in Duluth. But I was a *compadrito* too, a street-corner man in the *arrabales* of Buenos Aires and Montevideo where we would dance the tango alone under the gas lamps the way I will again. Alone in my limousine with the luggage racks, only I and my tears know the romantic illusion that drives the tango. I cruise on, love hardened, *endurecido*.

IV

Afternoon . . . yet twilight in an apartment where the table is set for love. Throwing off my high-heeled shoes and tight-fitting pants, I loosen the corset I wear for the back. Over hose, corset, and sleeveless T-shirt, I don the flower-print robe of my leisure hours.

Two candles flicker by his photo above the fainting couch. He was the greatest tango singer. "Gardel . . . Gardel. Look, I am weeping."

The object of my love, Mrs. Kovanic, lives three doors down. How was her morning?

"Dearest," I call through the door. "It is your José. Won't you answer?"

"Mr. *Keeto!*" Mrs. Laverdiere says when she sees me. "Stand up and knock! Don't peek through a keyhole!"

"Gracious Mrs.," I say.

Below my robe, two white kneecaps above the support hose.

"But where is Mrs. Kovanic?" I ask.

"In the Activities Room."

When I take the elevator down, my beloved, stopping her bridge game, asks, "What do you want?"

"How vulgar," Edith Bischoff says. "He can't even dress for Activities."

"Look at his teeth," says Judith Blundella.

"You're going to join the talent show, Joe, aren't you?" asks Helga Youngblood.

"I will enter in the dance category . . . a contact dance, sensual and tantalizing! The tango was once called 'the reptile of the brothel,' which is where you *all* belong!"

V

In the morning I telephone my hostess Joyce again.

"I will have to do a magnificent thing to win Mrs. Kovanic," I say. "Dearest Joyce, for the talent hunt show, will you help me?"

"It's not like you coming in off schedule. Don't your lumbago—"

"I wear a corset. I'll bring you baked goods, money," I tell her, getting my things ready, my tango records.

As she puts on the hi-fi, I, the master, begin with a walking step. "There are violins. Do you hear?"

"Yes, the *orquesta típica*. Listen. Are we in Buenos Aires, my friend?" Joyce says.

"Time has been stolen and we are young again," I tell her. "Now bend to me. We make the tango ours. Now bend," I say, "and— Ahhh!" I yell as I hear the cracking.

VI

She has to drive, friends and *muchachos*. I cannot straighten up on the way home.

"Don't the corset and hot water bottle help?" she asks in the limo.

"Ah," I say. "How we stole the time today."

"How're you going to dance, José Keeto? How? What kind of presentation is this gonna make on Friday night?"

"I will," I say, "for I am love-hardened and will dance without a corset!"

"You forgot my dance pay," Joyce says when she calls early the next morning.

"I will, dearest. Give me time. Two hundred dollars is *mucho dinero.*"

"To hell with your back," she says as though she has been drinking.

VII

Bent over to the waist, I must look up to Mrs. Kovanic's door. "Mrs. Kov—," I say at noon.

"What?"

"You hear my whisper then, dearest?"

"It's that retired baker," she calls to someone, a gentleman, inside.

"Please to pardon me, Mrs. Kovanic, but did you say 'Gilly' is in here?"

"It's no business of yours."

"But dearest Mrs. Kovanic, a whisper here, a caress there. Who knows where nights will lead us?"

"Get out," she says.

VIII

"Gimme the two hundred dollars," Joyce says again when she telephones.

"Please not to call, Joyce. I'm practicing dips and glides. I'll give you extra. My life savings. Just please not to call. Please just to come Friday for our show."

As I rest, *muchachos,* dear Mrs. Laverdiere fills the hot water bottle. "How, Joe, are you going to dance? You may as well forget the tango will ever win that old fool Pearl Kovanic over."

"In Argenti—"

"C'mon. You're from right here. A baker. The buns, remember, Joe?"

"Please to be wrong, Mrs. Laverdiere. In my Argentina, we have a word, *endurecido,* which means we mask our feelings. Maybe once we were deceived in love. But now no more. Now we are love-hardened. We command the woman. The man who gives in to his feelings, he is a *gil,* a fool, and love-softened, which is *reblandecido.* And that's why I dance. To show her and her 'Gilly.'"

IX

Bent in pain, I sit alone in the twilight of a Wednesday, sipping brandy, thinking of men with knives concealed in their boots, thinking of their posturing, their honor.

On Thursday I cleanse my dentures, trim my moustache, oil the wheels of my wheelchair for grace of movement. My back is so sore I must ride the wheelchair Mrs. Laverdiere has brought up from the storeroom. The only one left down there, it has enormous, antique wheels, a cane back and seat. Ah, the glamorous tango! They will expect it of me. From an antique wheelchair, how does a precious señor do an El Sharón Promenade? How does such a señor perform an attractive walking step?

X

All day Friday my diet is slight . . . a sip of sherry, a quarter of a wiener sandwich to invigorate me. I am the dream of the poor *porteños* who work in the warehouses along the River La Plata. The candles flicker, "Por Una Cabeza" plays. Music from the Night of Stars flickers through the summer air. It is time, I think.

I bless myself, begin to dress for those who desire me, the poor of the *arrabals* where I, too, was raised. I wear a lap quilt. Hat of my country? Yes. High-heeled tango shoes? Yes. Ruffled shirt? Yes. Knife beneath the lap quilt? Yes.

Down the darkened passage, I roll in the wheelchair of the high back whose wheels click as I go. "*Mina*, I have had many many such as you. '*Verás que todo es mentira*,'" I say as I pass her room. I hear the clapping downstairs. How will I stand it?

"Where is he?" they will wonder. "Has anyone seen the masterful Señor Keeto? It is getting so late," they will say.

"Ah, the world is evil," I sing in the elevator. I think of Ciriaco Ortiz, the *bandoneón* player, of his Orquesta Tipica "Los Provincianos"—the abrupt movements thought too crude for the ballroom, the introduction of the smaller ensembles. Ah, Eduardo Arelas, Francisco Canaros. Where are you now for a precious señor?

Joyce is waiting. I have slain many in the creole knife duels of the old days. I posture, raise an eyebrow to her in the lobby. "Hah," I clutch the knife under the blanket.

"A wheelchair?" Joyce says. "Jeezus, I could see a walker, but a wheelcha—? You tryin' the sympathy angle?"

"Please to rock me back and forth when I say 'dip step,' dearest Joyce," I tell her.

The Activities Room is dark, bookcases and tables pushed aside. Dying for love, they all buzz and swoon for the poor baker Keeto whose buns rose. I hear the sighing of women who will never dance the tango. Framed in the light of the door, they see me, a slender, mysterious figure in a wheelchair.

"Ladies and gentlemen . . . From the pampas, here on our variety stage," says the manager, "is our master *tanguero* . . . our own Joe Ke-e-e-to, Apartment 908."

"Joyce, you *must*," I say. "I will pay you. But now . . . here in the dance to help me."

"You better have your checkbook," she whispers, pushing me into the spotlight.

As I stare into the Buenos Aires night, I pause to light a cheroot. I think of the time I have stolen for my life, of the *tempo rubato* of living to near seventy. The people of the slums come to see their idol Keeto on his last grand tour, for which he has chosen fittingly "*La Cumparsita*," the lament of a man abandoned by the woman he loved. I stamp out the cheroot, see far over La Plata to Punta del Este. In front of me, the laughing whores. Left arm straight, right arm embracing an imaginary partner, Joyce behind me ready to push.

"Damn you," she says over the high cane back.

"Slow now. Slow . . . slow . . . quick . . . quick," I tell her. "Wheel me this way, that way. Dip me, glide me as I bid farewell like a swan."

"Money," she says into my shoe-polished head.

"I have no money," I say as the *bandoneónes* play, the wheelchair beginning to roll.

I throw kisses to the adoring. Ah, how smooth the chair!

"*Corté*. Now *corté* and dip me," I say.

"He owes me money," she says to Mrs. Laverdiere in the crowd.

"Please to dip me. It is my farewell. No one listen to her. Please to watch my Walking Step. I am masterful. I am El Keeto! Tango me forever, my darlings."

She rocks me, hurries me in circles.

"What?" I say, shoe polish dripping from my forehead.

She tips me on one wheel.

"Aiee—! *No mas,*" I say. "Please to stop now, Joyce. Someone please to make her stop . . . please to bring me roses."

"Now a Conga. One-two-three *kick.*" Raising her knee to the back of the wheelchair, she aims me for the rubber plant. I reverse out. I Copa . . . Habeñara. "*Mina!*" I say.

As I reach for her to taste my knife, she jitterbugs Keeto, the great *tanguero!* My fans shriek. Over goes the wheelchair, my whole wiener-encased life going down before me. Dante Linyera . . . Vicente Greco . . . Taystee Bakery *mi Buenos Aires.*

"Pants!" they yell. "Pants! Get us out! Turn on the lights! The old fruitcake—!" They yell for my glide, my promenade. All over, Argentines requesting, *desiring,* the mystery. "It is he finally come . . . Keeto Pants-less!" says the manager as he writes on the blackboard, "PINOCHLE CANCELED TONIGHT."

"Betrayed," I whisper to the blood and sand of this tile floor, my only lover. How near to my moustache it lies. "'*Verás que nada es amor* . . . You'll see that nothing ends in love, that the world doesn't give a damn.'"

"Someone," I moan, the lap quilt over my head. "I can't get up . . . lumbago. Please—?" But the wheels of the chair that danced, they spin. The records, they spin—"*La Cumparsita,*" "*El Choclo,*" "*Retintin.*" I taste the bitter sand, feel the edge of a knife meant for Joyce the whore and for Pearl Kovanic. That *mina* Pearl with her fiery eyes, how I held her once and dropped her, how she cursed and laughed. Now my naked heels dig into the carpet as I think of the times I strode into Buenos Aires where there were many, many women to wrong you.

XI

In the morning, no one having helped me, I crawl to where the early birds of the Saturday watercolor painting class can observe nature in its raw uncovered state.

"Is that a bald eagle . . . a cowbird?" they say, filing past me.

"Looks more like a little baby water pipit. We'll have to paint it."

"Draped or undraped?"

I am partly hidden by the lap quilt but not the centipedes, one on my lip, the other hanging lifeless between my legs, limp . . . lifeless. I, Señor Keeto, one-time "*tanguero* to the stars!"

"What a pity," Mrs. Laverdiere says in the afternoon when they have gotten me to bed. "A pity, abandoned like he was. All the dancing he did. I'm gonna miss you."

"Miss me? Where am I going? To Argentina?"

How cruel the nights, how heartless women who will not accept my banana nut bread. They no longer crave my baking.

"Don't go near him if he's got a lap quilt on," they whisper.

"I am a humbled Keeto," I say, wheeling the floor from noon to night, but no one helps me. I knock on doors, disturb lovers in their slumbers. At midnight I am here doing the dance of the antique wheelchairs. At three A.M. Night in, night out.

When all is quiet I begin again. First the entrance into the grand hall, then down to the janitor's closet. "Please to come out. Please to observe, Mrs. Kovanic, Mrs. Laverdiere. The precious señor is here," I call along the way, wheeling, spinning.

"Shoo!" they whisper and slam apartment doors on a lonely rake in the middle of the night.

When he finds me down at the fire exit, the manager says, "We called Social Services. They said they'll help. We're giving you your notice."

"No, please to not treat me so. Please to come in. Hear the music, have a bun."

"*Nada*," he says. "Sorry it has to be this way, but you were never right for the place, Joe."

"Is there nothing a precious señor can do?"

"Yeah, you can start with a different color shoe polish in the new place and wear underpants!"

The apartment now is empty, *muchachos,* cleaned out. Ah, it is no good. No hi-fi, no tables, no chairs. Now they are moving me to a rest home for my lumbago . . . my cardboard suitcases, my shopping bag of Gardel records. On my last day, I sit before the open door and dream. I have danced once too often in my wheelchair in the hall, they say. Hours are vacant. I whisper "Jalousie," my favorite tango, as dearest Mrs. Kovanic passes by.

"Too much *rubato,*" she says to "Gilly."

"A little tetched in the noggin," he says, tapping the side of his head.

The lovers laugh and go their way as I wheel out. I do not bother to think of their happiness. In the twilight of my life, I stop in the middle of the ninth floor and think of my youth in the Argentine and how, like the antique wheelchair I ride, my horse was a good one and Gardel and I two *muchachos* who loved to tango.

The Polkaholics

I

A polkaholic lived next door. "I geev you neekel," she said one day. Withdrawing from the agony of polka addiction, she was shivering in her *babushka* and brown coat. She wore heavy black shoes with thick heels, nylons rolled to her knees, an old workman's belt around her coat waist.

She'd knotted the nickel in a piece of dishcloth. I raked her ditch, burned the garbage. Through the screen door I saw her giving in to her compulsions.

"Eat!" she called. She came out with a bowl. "*Czarnina* good for you. Eat, then dance with me!" she said, her huge breasts heaving from dancing the "Iron Range Polka" by herself.

"Thank you," I said to Mrs. Pomerinski.

When I saw her ax in the chopping block, her duck Aloosh's blood in the *czarnina*, I took off, running through Redlinskis', Falkowskis', and Fronckiewiczs' yards where the lake wind blew ore dust from the docks. Polka abuse was—still is—our number one social ill. With all the old time "polka parties" on radio and the accordion players working cheap for a Whoopee John record, Superior's the place for polka addicts. It's easy to relapse here. In 1991 I have the 78 rpm "Milwaukee Polka" that Lawrence Duchow and His Red River Orchestra played in 1949.

The places I ran through still have grain, ore, and coal dust on them. It streaks the brown and green asphalt shingles of the houses. The dust is one of the cruel things about Superior. Another is weather that makes the people and their buildings ugly. In this neighborhood in the Polka Standard Time of my youth were also a drugstore, bank, bakery, library, butcher shop, and four taverns, one called "The Warsaw." "GATEWAY TO POLKA COUNTRY" read signs on the streets, but all my sister and I ever wanted was to get out of Polka Country.

A local disc jockey, Ad Dzuniak, was broadcasting music from a 1¢ Sale at the drugstore the day I escaped Mrs. Pomerinski. When my old man walked up from the flour mill in his work dungarees, asking to hear the same "Milwaukee Polka" I still have on record, for one minute he was famous. It's hard to imagine how his arms and legs could grow so weak. *Where can I turn the loop antenna on our old Wards Airline radio to bring in your signal? I wonder.* He looked around. "Come, Edek, dance with me," he said.

We went down the aisle by laxatives, up past cod liver oil, people laughing at Stash and his son. Forward and back he dipped me. Hopping past the mercurochrome display, he swung me toward the health and beauty department. "Yoo-hoo-hoo," he yelled. I whooped "Hoo-yaa-yaa." Here was this tall, rough man in his miller's cap dancing his kid through the trusses and canes.

"T'anks, t'anks," he said to the disc jockey, to everyone else as he polkaed me out. Down by the tavern where my father had done too much "Chicago Push" style polkaing the night before, the postman came struggling past us. "*Ladies Home Journals . . . National Geography,*" he was muttering, crossing himself, but we kept on dancing. When we passed Mrs. Pomerinski's there was a new duck in the yard.

Why am I telling all this? Whatever happened to us, father and son? We used to listen to the polka, dance down streets. Back then my sister was on speaking terms with him, but when everything went smash between them, she danced out as fast as she could. Their dance haunts me, too, hers and my father's.

After that she had nothing to come home for. She'd once worn plaid dresses and had honey-colored hair that covered her face when she leaned forward. At fifteen she started hating polka and its emissary to our house, however. Stash was not a bad guy, but everything had to be just so around the place, that was all—school shoes lined here, play shoes put there.

"Your clothes ironed?" he'd ask in Polish.

"Yes," we'd answer.

"Do the dishes then," he'd say.

The polka jamboree would be playing on the Wards Airline radio with the built-in loop antenna. He wouldn't talk. He was thin, strong. He might bring you to the kitchen cupboard, put lard on your lips. Back then in the Dark Ages of

Polka Country, USA, watch out if those huge, rough fingers grabbed you behind the neck. "*Cicha woda brzegi rwie,*" he'd say.

When they'd see the old man go with his lunchbox, seniors from the high school would call. They'd telephone as late as eleven o'clock if he was on the night shift.

"She went to bed," I'd say.

"Who with?" they'd say.

Once when she was sixteen, my sister hid behind her hair. "Eddie, Eddie, come 'ere," she said. When I listened to the telephone, two boys were singing Skip and Flip's "Cherry Pie." They were professionals, it sounded like. She met the one with the guitar under the Northern Pacific ore dock that runs high over the East End neighborhood. Beneath this wooden dock, red ore dust drifts in the ditches, makes the earth rusty. Even three miles inland, the Lake Superior winds blow across stock-piled ore. She was red with the dust when she got home.

II

In those innocent days, girls knotted their scarves at the chin. Only practiced fingers undid the knots. My father, being King of Polka, of course, could undo her scarves every time. Like he needed action as much as the high school seniors, he'd grumble, "You staying in" when she'd be getting ready for a joyride. Let's say maybe his reason was they announced a new "Six-Year Plan" in Poland, or one of his favorite saint's days was coming up, "Waldemara's" or "Pankracego's," somebody my sister never heard of.

"Goddamn it," I'd hear her saying in her room.

She'd take off her charm bracelet, pull the wadded Bee-man's gum from the dresser mirror. Readjusting her scarf, she'd head downstairs again chewing her gum.

"Please, Pa," she'd say, "can't I go out?"

He'd slap horseradish on his sandwich.

"You stay in."

"You can't make a person against her will."

In the living room, Ma'd throw up her hands, cross herself. "It's night, Marysha," Ma'd tell her. "Where you go?"

Stash would have on his clean work pants, a sleeveless T-shirt. If his coughing worsened from the flour dust he breathed all day, he'd sit on the edge of the bathtub and close the door. "*Psia krew!*" you'd hear him say, which is a Polish curse. Was it for Mary's benefit who was sitting in the front room watching the seniors drive past, or mine who'd gotten his nose dislocated sticking up for her when one of my friends said she drove around in "sex feens'" cars?

When Stash had a night off from work she got freed, though. Maybe some new button-box player or polka trio was performing at the Moose Club that Stash and Wanda, my mother, had to hear. I wonder how far my sister Marysha went when Stash and Wanda were doing the "Hupa Shupa." You bet both parents were there when the accordions started up.

Polkaholics have this profile: the women, swollen legs; the men, strong legs and backs but bad lungs. When he was in the Merchant Service Stash cleaned ships' engines with carbon tetrachloride. He'd *earned* his lungs, the way I did my nose. "No ventilation," he'd tell me about those days, "and t'er I was, a full-fledged, certified polkaholic, breathing chemicals like it was powdered sugar on *pączki.*"

"That heavy dough, those sweet fillings . . . I hate all Polish pastries," my sister would say within hearing. "No wonder you people are all so . . . sturdy. I hate polka! I hate accordion!"

After fifteen years at sea, even more hacking up flour dust, Stash got a Lip Ivo and two Vaporubs at a 1¢ Sale and a smart mouth for a daughter at home. The Lip Ivo was great, though. It got us out of the Lard Age. It wasn't the taste or feel of lard when he smeared it on, for there was nothing to that; it was the way he did it, how rough and hard his fingers were. That was a lousy thing to do.

A year after those arguments, after the lard and the fights, something else happened in Stanley Patulski's great life. Once when he was walking home on East 2nd Street after the night shift at Fredericka Flour, Frankie Yankovic and His Yanks drove by. "Edek, Edek," Stash said when he saw me. I was heading to serve Mass. It was some obscure saint's day, the Feast of St. Wiesława. I'd spotted the old man's white miller's cap, his work dungarees, his lunch pail a half-mile away. As he came closer, you could see flour dust on his face. After an eight-hour shift, he'd come home and scrape paint or cut the grass. All he did was work. Probably the Yankovic band had been traveling from the Upper Peninsula to the Iron Range. Asleep, they maybe never saw Stash wave his lunch pail at them, but at least he saw the bus and had had a brush with greatness.

My sister, who'd graduated now to counter help at S. S. Kresge's uptown, came home from work. "Big deal, you saw Frankie Yankovic," she said. "You act like it's Frankie Lyman and the Teenagers."

"*Kto się lubi, ten się czubi* . . . Those who like each other, peck at each other," he'd said.

The next day I was laughing with my friends about his speaking Polish when he let me have it. I rode with Marysha to the Kresge's uptown photo booth to document life's cruelty in Superior's polka slums. Slums or not, life was good. We had a radio, even though my sister wanted rock 'n roll. Eddie "Edek" Patulski sits in this photo with a black eye for laughing at his father. On each photo my face has no smile. The light brown hair is wetted and combed, the black eye, the dazed eyes, stare out at the light, the nose I earned twists one way then back.

"Take some extra photos, Edek. Put them in your graduation announcements for him to remember you by."

"*Nie szkodzi* . . . it doesn't matter," I told my sister who went behind the counter to get me a Coke. "I don't graduate for a long time."

He was sorry for laying into me, he said a few days after the photos. "*Niema dymu bez ognia*, Edek. 'No smoke without fire,'" he said. He kissed my head, gave me a Vaporub.

For three or four years after that, he worked seven days a week. In appreciation for his service, he got a wristwatch from the mill. He hardly had breath to walk to the head table to shake the boss's hand. He didn't wear the stupid miller's cap, thank God. He had brains enough to put on a suitcoat for the party. "You can be confident your new Lord Elgin will stand up under the stress of normal wear. It has a Shock Resistant Guarantee," the card with the watch read.

Sweepers and oilers applauded. Here was a guy shaky on his pins, who'd given eighteen years to the firm. Because of "polka lung" he was getting out. Embarrassed about retiring, what could Stash do? Your breathing flour dust, your drafty halls, your cigarette smoking, your yelling "Yoo-hoo-hoo" will bring this on every time. So will breathing coal and ore dust—or carbon tetrachloride if you're cleaning cylinder heads in the belly of an ocean freighter. I think polkaholics breathe them all. I heard of a guy who worked in a tire factory. Everything in his house smelled of rubber. I heard of a Polack who worked in a chemical bath. Every day for forty years he rode a city bus to the end of the line, got off, then hitchhiked two miles to work, all of this to dip his hands in chemicals for ten hours. When he retired his lungs were so shot he couldn't leave his bed. Have you heard of Stash Patulski, whose wife was Wanda, whose kids are Eddie and Marysha?

III

As I tell Stash's story I realize what's left of the old, ugly neighborhood now. It went away like my sister. It went off the air like Bobby Oro's polka show does on WDSE at midnight before "The Star-Spangled Banner."

Once Stash retired, life went downhill. One day you're feeling his fingers grab your neck; the next you're wondering where is the old man's strength that he can't dance anymore. With him home at the Polka Hall of Fame, my sister, who was twenty-one when she left, really had no peace. That poor, foolish man would put on his miller's cap like he missed work, sit out in the shade of the elm tree, and dream about the Yankovic boys.

"Where you go?" he'd ask her when she'd take his car.

"The market, Pa. You don't want me to push all these groceries home in a cart. Going to get your sauerkraut. What else do you want?"

Tightening her scarf, she'd put on lipstick, readjust the rearview mirror, turn the station to Buddy Knox's "Party Doll" or James Brown's "Night Train." I've never had a party doll, never been married, never been to "Atlanta, Gaa-gia" like in James Brown's song.

When my sister returned from the market, Stash would complain that he liked Frank's Sauerkraut in the can, not in the jar . . . that he preferred Polish rye.

The night I graduated from high school, the night she'd been anticipating a few years before in the photo booth, was the night my sister got the hell out. "I can write Polish good enough to spell 'ASSHOLE,'" she wrote in my graduation card. She included my photo with Stash's handiwork on my face. Stanislaus Patulski definitely needed Shock Resistance to get through that. "How do you insure against daughters like her?" Stash wondered to my mother.

I gave her flow-ers
I gave her can-dy
All that she said was
"Thanks, they're dan-dy."
Hu-La-La-La-La
Hu-La-La-La-La

You wonder what makes guys like Stash do this to their kids. He had everything—a house with gray shingles, a little yard between us and Vankiewicz's next door, a '56 Chevy, a good baker in my mother Wanda, two kids, a phonograph, a Wards Airline radio. If he didn't want to do anything but listen to "Hu-La-La-La-La Polka" all day, he could have. It was the lungs and the dreams that got him, I guess. He wanted my sister to go to Mass every day, to Forty Hours' Devotion, to have her throat blessed for St. Blaise's, to receive ashes for Ash Wednesday, to give up cherry pie for Lent, to get a palm for Palm Sunday, to observe Rogation Days. He dreamt of her getting a good education, then clerking at the NP or maybe hooking on at Fredericka Flour Mill if she was lucky. Was this so much to ask? Instead, she sailed out of here for good one night in some guy's car.

After that I wanted to see what it was like to be a polka-holic. I figured I owed it to the old country and Stash to see what he'd gone through to become such a jerk as to force his own daughter away from home. He got me a job on the water-front humping grain doors, seventy-pound wood slabs that keep the wheat in boxcars. I worked with the empties. This was before the railroad started using covered hoppers, C-9s. The best I figure, to be a polkaholic you have to carry a lunch pail with a thermos of coffee, work all day, smash your hands, ruin your back, come home, have a beer, wash your neck, get things painted on the house, sweep the sidewalk, cut the grass. Saturdays you sleep a little in the afternoon, then eat a good supper, down a *pączki* or two, read the *Pol-American Journal,* then go to Confession. Thick neck and arms straining your suitcoat, afterwards you drive your well-kept Chev or Ford to the VFW or the Polish Lodge on Winter Street, then polka like hell, Stash Patulski and like-minded men and women, polka like it's your last night on earth, like it don't matter your lungs and dreams are shot.

IV

Eventually, he moved upstairs. My Ma wanted me to have a life of my own so they gave me the downstairs. The house has an attic, two floors, and a basement. He had my Ma, and he had a record player. Coming home after work—I was twenty-four now and doing hard labor down on the waterfront—I'd say, "You up there, Stan and Wanda? This wouldn't be Superior, Wisconsin, without a polka. Here we go, 'Ee-I-Oh.'" I'd set down the tone arm on the downstairs hi-fi, crank up the volume, dance upstairs to them. As the accordions brought tears to our eyes, all three of us would yell "Yoo-hoo-hoo."

> Join in the fun;
> Get your troubles on the run,
> Sing-in' Ee-I Ee-I Ee-I Oh ——
> Brighten your days
> With this catchy little phrase:
> Ee-I Ee-I Ee-I Oh ——
> It's got the beat
> That will sweep you off your feet:
> Ee-I Ee-I Ee-I Oh ——
> Let's all relax
> Like polkamaniacs. . . .

"He likes that one," Ma would say over the music. "How he used to sing, Edek. It's sad."

With the next number, I'd grab her. With the "polka hop" style, both of you face forward. One arm behind the other's back, you catch the beat. Bouncing, skipping, you twirl your partner under your outstretched arms, dance forward a few more steps. All around the living room Ma and I hopped and jumped to the music from downstairs, tears coming down my face as I saw my Pa trying to remember how to polka.

"Give us a 'Hoo-yaa-yaa' for old time's sake, Papa," I'd yell. He'd be on the couch. Afghan over him, legs on the footstool, he'd look up, honestly try a good old-fashioned "hoo-hoo-hoo." Then he realized it was no good, that everybody had deserted him, because when he opened his eyes again and stared at me, Edek his boy, all he could do was shake his head.

"Why you don't come upstairs more often?" he would ask.

My Ma would say, "Come see your father more, Edek."

He'd cross himself, try to get up from the couch, curse the strength the wheat'd taken. "You're no good son," he'd say. "You do nothink."

This is what I mean. Right before you, he was becoming a stupid, senile polkaholic while his son was a success in the world of business and industry.

"Why you don't come up?" he'd ask again. "You forget me? Your mother?"

"Gotta look after things all the time," I'd say.

"You don't look after nothink," he'd say.

Him being too much to look at in his sorry state, I'd go downstairs to fix my supper. I'd say at the top of my lungs, "You want 'Pennsylvania Polka?' 'Hu-La-La-La-La Polka?' You want to look at the old map of Marseilles from your sailing days? You like to do that."

If he didn't answer, I'd leave. "I won't bring you nothing then, Pa, if you're going to act like that," I'd say in the early darkness. "*Wszystkie stare czasy są dobre* . . . All times are good when old. Enjoy them."

From the window he'd watch. I'd hear his crying as I went under the streetlights to the church where I'd utter prayers of gratitude for my own great and successful life. Later, after a night at the Warsaw, I'd turn up the volume on the downstairs phonograph at home. Drunk, I'd yell, "All your problems have one solution . . . Join the Polka Revolution!"

"Edek," I'd hear him calling. "Why you don't come up?"

"Why?" I'd say to myself. "Why'd you hit me when things got tough? Why'd you wreck your lungs? Why'd everything have to be just so around here? Why'd you never want me to be a Polack?" At my desk I would say up to him the only Polish words that meant anything to me: "*Nie ma Ojca* . . . I have no father." Look, I have done okay for myself. Who needs an old man like you? I'd think. It was how you went about everything, Stashu. Jesus, didn't you hear yourself yelling? *Nie ma Ojca.* Look, I live in your house. I drink at the Warsaw. I'm drunk. I have no party doll . . . never been west of Duluth. When I tell you I'm going to Mass, I really head for the donut shop. What's become of your son, Stash? How many donuts can I eat during a High Mass? In November when Forty Hours' Devotion rolls around, I gain twenty pounds by not going to church. I lie to the priest at confession the way I lie to you. I lie about being Polack. I eat beef and ham on days of fast and abstinence. I wipe off my Ash Wednesday ashes from my forehead. I always check my shirt for ashes. *Nie ma Ojca.*

After midnight when I'd sober up, when the coughing above me stopped, when the house finally settled in for the night, I'd find Stash with my mother's rosary. His old lungs struggling for one more prayer, he'd say, "*Święta Maryo, Matko Boża, Matko i Opiekunko moja, oddaję się w Twoją opiekę . . .*" He always prayed the Blessed Virgin would restore Superior to its former grandeur when the shipyards were busy, when the docks had the best year in history, and when the polkas and obereks rang till dawn in the crazy streets of the East and North Ends.

When my sister came home once every two or three years, I didn't tell her about the Cold War between the *Amerikański* downstairs and the Polack upstairs. I was thirty-three, getting Stan back for the times he'd forced his will on us, principally on Ma and Mary, though I got my share of times we had to tiptoe about because Stash was resting for the night shift, years smeared with lard, years he pushed me around the room for lying on the couch in daytime, for listening to Joey Dee's "Peppermint Twist," for not kissing bread if I accidentally dropped a piece from my plate.

After she left, the house would grow quiet again. She didn't wear scarves, just a lot of makeup now. She had her own Buick. At my desk, one light illuminating the insurance papers I work with, I'd listen to Bobby Oro's polka show on WDSE radio and figure actuarial tables into the night. Long ago, maybe during the autumn after my sister took off, a midnight storm sent sleet through our roof. A hundred-year rain and snow in mid-October, it came in along the upstairs ceiling. The pattern in the room he slept in most of his life (even before my parents moved upstairs it was Stash's bedroom), the pattern was like nothing I'd seen before, like something caught midway between an old country and Polka Town, USA. This was Stanislaus "Stash" Patulski himself, a mysterious pattern . . . my old man who was too tough for his own good, who worked too hard all his life like he couldn't enjoy America. Strict, old-fashioned, he should've lived in Poland and trained up a son to shovel cowshit into a cart with wooden wheels. I'd escaped laboring after a while, now had a better job, my own office.

"Insurance business not good tonight?" Stash would ask when I'd come up once in a while. Struggling for air, he'd lay against a pillow. My mother would putter around.

"Not so good, Pa."

"Whad you gonna do at your age? How old are you now?"

"Thirty-three now. I don't know. Maybe I'll go to work at the Warsaw," I'd tell him. It was a joke.

"Go to the mill, sweep flour like a fool then," he'd say. Disappointed, he'd turn away from me.

"Look what I brought like in the old days, Stash. Something you'll like from the market."

When he turned around I'd dip in my thumb and smear some over my lips.

"Too bad Mary ain't here. How about you, Stash? Your lips feeling a little chapped tonight in need of lard?"

"Why you do this, Edek?" he'd ask.

When you don't really think it is, time is passing, dreams passing, dreams for me and Marysha that made him trudge to work for eighteen years so we'd have the good life. If you have to go through this as a kid . . . I don't know.

"What you hear from her?" Ma'd ask.

"She's doing real good for herself," I'd say.

V

During the last lonely years of Stash's life he'd work the crossword, eat his shredded wheat, then blow up a balloon to see how much life was left. When he was done Ma'd attempt it. She had better lungs. As soon as I got home from the life insurance business that in reality wasn't going so hot, she'd tell me, "He's failing, Edek." Then *he'd* start. It was a residue from the old days that he felt the need to yell. If the pork hocks I bought were tough, if I smoked around the house, if I had one too many and played an oberek when he wasn't in the mood, he'd yell, "Care for thees house, dammit. Look . . . the storm windows."

I, a self-made Edek, could withstand the eventuality of Stanislaus's death, I thought. Sure, I could face the loneliness of Polka Land easy. Sometimes rain seeped in the basement window, trailed down walls, settled in pools on the floor where my childhood bicycle stood. Minerals clogged the pipe that went into the humidifier tray in the furnace. When he couldn't get downstairs Stash only guessed at what was happening to me and him.

"You know what hurts worst, Stash, was when you called me '*Gapa.*' Your own kid. The nuns heard it."

"A '*gapa*' is a gawker," he'd say.

His gray head resting against the back of the couch, he'd wave at me while he caught his breath. He was not so tall, I thought. Let him try a sucker punch now.

"You always complaining," he'd say. "What did we have? Look, you got a good job, a nice house downstairs. You got a church and a health. You don't have to walk to the flour mill no more. You got t' good life."

The first-rate millhand, Stash now wore a corset to steady his back against coughing. He'd hack from morning to night. Bent over, he'd heave at the wheat dust he'd breathed all those years I was gaping and gawking, marveling at the wonderful future a St. Adalbert's grade school education held for me.

Sometimes I didn't see him for a week. When the loneliness got too great, I'd go up and polka. Why did I cling to the old man one floor up in this house whose windows looked out on Lake Superior, the long, blue edge? Sometimes when him and Ma saw me, their ungrateful Edek, looking up from the yard, they'd gaze down. We'd stare at each other. He'd point down from the window, say, "You've ruined the best years of our life."

More and more the priest came over. My Dad's hands fumbled for Shock Resistant Guarantees. Others visited. The only ones missing from Stan Patulski's sickbed were his son and willful daughter.

Toward the end, the *Amerikański* won the Cold War when his, the *Amerikański's*, mother called in perfect English one night: "He's dying."

I looked out, put on a late-night radio show. During the hours after midnight, the nurse went up to him.

"How is he?" I asked from the bottom of the stairs as the nurse telephoned the hospital.

"Done dancing, I'm afraid."

"And Ma?"

"Come up and see."

Upstairs, I dusted Pa's phonograph for him, wandered through the rooms fixing things as right as I could, though they'd kept the place pretty clean themselves. How he'd fretted over the pattern of a hundred-year rain. Like all our lives, it's an act of God.

"Been a while since I've been up," I, a success in life, told the doctor when he arrived.

Stash's hair was combed so nice. Ma'd probably shaved him too, or maybe one of the polkamaniacs from Fredericka Flour when I was out selling insurance. With the men from the mill or the Kosciuszko Lodge, Stash was always happy. He'd accept a shave from them. Now I needed to talk to someone. I had years of things to say. Why had he hated Mary for being a party doll and me for laughing at a language I never knew? Everything upstairs was so clean at the hour of my father's death. I brought up a phrase book I'd gotten a year before. Sitting by his bed where he could hardly breathe, I muttered things like *"Nie szkodzie . . .* it doesn't matter" and *"Dziękuje za pomoc . . .* Thank you for your help." Then I kissed his head. When he died the nurse fixed Stanley's arms on his chest, put in his teeth. My old man, the Polka King, was gone forever.

VI

Seeing my father lying in state a few days later like the commander-in-chief of the Polish Army, I thought for a fleeting moment that Stash, who really *had* done something with his life by working, by raising a family, by paying his bills on time, by keeping the house up, by going to Mass, should have worn the Military Cross the Polish Army gives for bravery. Mind you, it was only a fleeting moment I thought this. Waiting in the church, at the cemetery, was every living polkaholic in Superior. They were standing there as they had for years at weddings and funerals, old people you wouldn't even know were still alive if you hadn't sold them a life insurance policy: Augie Fronckiewicz, Louie Majewski, Ad Stasiak, Stephania Wozniak, Albin Szymczyk, Stella Stranko, Jan Bachinski, Paweł Chudzik, Anna Miernicki, Steven Malinowski. Heavy men, broad-shouldered . . . women in *babushkas* and gray coats, muttering prayers. They fit the profile all right. These polkaholics, I bet, never missed a beat. "Tell him not to dance too much." That's what the doctor and nurse said were Stan's dying words to me. "Hu-La-La-La-La" were my last words to him.

Later, a month after, I found an old dictionary. Written in pencil on the pages in the front were words like "*parowe ruri* (steam pipes)," words which he'd used in the engine room of merchant ships in the North Atlantic. What was written in back? The words you could make out told about places he'd been as a young man. Sometimes when I look at my father's Polish I understand these distances. Along the shore were signal beacons that could have lighted our way against the acts of God.

At the funeral, my sister, who'd gone to Buffalo, then Syracuse over the years and was now selling real estate in Oswego, told me she wanted no part of the manor, so I inherited it. Under my care the stairs separated from the wall: all the way up, they pulled gently away like the heart of my dying father. When I was young and life good, he had come up those stairs, sat on my bed, told me about time and how you couldn't recover it. Downstairs I'd hear Ma listening to the polka jamboree. He had pulled the covers close about me then, said, "Good night, Edek." Later I realized that time is inside of you like an inland sea. Memories of shores never fade.

Now that they're gone I talk to Stash and Wanda, especially to the old man. "I should throw out your dusty clothes, Pa, your favorite polka albums. I should get your room fixed a little better for you." But instead of doing these things I make tapes on a tape recorder and play them back to myself, maybe to him if he's out there listening.

At night I check the clock. Trying to assess the contours of time and sea, I turn on the radio, call the phone company for the exact time. "8:07 P.M., November 16, 1991," the voice says. Listening for a polka from Bobby Oro's radio show, winding my father's watch, thinking of my mother, once more I head into distant, timeless seas. Turning on the RECORD button to remember the moment in history when Poland and my parents were lost to me, I say, "Testing, testing . . . this is Edek, your son . . . one, two, three." Bobby Oro on WDSE then hits his listeners with a polka three-pack, my tape recorder's going, and once more on this northerly course there is just the darkness of a world ahead of me and I, Edek Patulski, dancing the minutes away.

The Tomb of the

Wrestlers

THE drugstore's postcards aren't accurate. They give aerial views of Superior, so you can't see the city close up. Sure, the sun was shining, but this isn't usually so. Sure, it's pretty in the country, but not in town.

Superior is a city that grows smaller the more they tear down. On a map the north and south shores of the lake meet to form what looks like an arrow point. We live at the tip. This and other arrows pierce us, but we don't leave. The area is called two things: the Arrowhead Region and the Head of the Lakes. If a person hears these names, he shouldn't get confused.

Here's a kind of word postcard you can't buy at the counter of Lignell's Drugs or the Globe News because I made it up. Imagine this: weeds that grow over rusted tracks . . . no diesels slowing for the crossings . . . no ore boat whistles ever piercing the foggy noon. Here's more on my postcard: berthed at the docks in town are these old ore boats rusting in the rain. The tracks leading to the docks rust. Two or three boats have been torn apart for scrap. Plenty others await the cutting torch. Not ten feet from the back door of my old man's tavern, three big ore boats rise up out of murky water. During bad weather they break loose and drift across the bay. Another berth holds Inland Steel Co. ships; another berth, Cleveland Cliffs Co. ships. Except for the rust and chipping paint, they're ready to carry ore from here to Buffalo. But steel work ain't good anymore. This is Superior, a town where the only thing left are the drinkers and drunks.

Please don't ask for my next two postcards at Lignell's Drugs or the Chamber of Commerce. One is of the Northern Pacific Ore Dock in East End. To my old man it's a concrete and steel palace stained all red with ore dust. The beams rise up, then give way to these concrete arches which support the tracks and the trains that used to run high up there when ore was being sent to Detroit and Cleveland. Nothing's going on there now . . .

The other postcard is of the bar. It's a word postcard signed by me, the artist. Outside hanging up over the door is a big neon heart of pink with a jagged break in it (my sign) and the words Heartbreak Hotel. A glass of beer's a quarter; a "bowl" of beer, fifty cents. Add thirty-five cents, you get a shot of whisky or brandy. Then what you're drinking is called a "boilermaker," "one 'n one," or a "bump 'n a beer." People inside know the terms: "shot glass," "bowl of beer," "bar tab," "bar rag," "bar time," "bump and a beer," or one hundred terms beginning with "bar" or "beer," like "bar salami" or "beer chaser." They tell each other how drunk they got. They yell at each other for falling off bar stools.

This is a kind of insider's map, the word postcards I've made up. Then there's the map of the inside of me, the map of my heart, which is a dark, spiritless series of hills because I know I'm never getting out of here. This much I haven't made up: I'm Bob Harris. Age nineteen. High School Grad. Brown Hair. Blue Eyes. Here is how a map of the heart works: My parents, in their early sixties, had me later in life when Ma retired and it was convenient for her. Kids called her "Mattress Back." I love her in spite of her work history. My old man's the one that causes the map to curl up at the edges. "You're always whorin' around on the boats like those Indian women," he says to me. "You're always getting picked up. Now you're workin' the Canadian boats," he says. He owns a bar, but he lies and drinks up most of what he makes. Then we're so poor he has to cheat the government out of the surplus food commodities or the fuel assistance money they provide to needy families.

If you're poor like we are because of the old man and if you go once a month for free flour and cheese at the Community Services Agency, you'll see the drinkers lining up across the street for a drink or three to get the day started. My old man's seen it all—meanness, public sin, men and women violating everything. So have I. My heart is a shattered neon sign. It should be put up outside Heartbreak Hotel to blink on and off in the fog. It's one hill after another. They're getting bigger, too. Now Ma's sick. She aches. "I'm too warm," she tells me when I come in at midnight one night. So I fold the blanket at her ankles, leaving only a thin sheet to cover her. "Now I'm chilled," she says. I pull the blanket back up and get another one, all the time wondering where in hell the old man is.

"Feeling better?" he says. It's 2:30 A.M. He didn't even know she was sick, and he comes in asking her that out of spite.

"Some better," she says.

She don't look good.

"Can I make a sandwich out of the commodity cheese Dad cheats the government out of, Ma?" I ask.

"She ain't hungry. Neither are you," he answers for her. He wants it for himself.

I know she irritates him. She has a corrosive effect on him. They get along, but there are times when he says he needs his freedom and just sleeps at the bar or passes out in the park. It's dreary having him home. He likes things in place. This evening, or morning, Ma is corroding his spirit. He's had too much Royal Bohemian beer. On the way home he said he'd looked forward to finding his Magda snoozing. He'd have kissed her, maybe cried a little, he told me. But here instead of a good sob over this old, broken down wh—, woman, and over himself, a hapless, drunken fool, he's had to play nursemaid.

(Another word postcard: I hope the poor, dear people of this town breathe smoke and soot up to the last; that their cries for beer go strangled by foghorns that never stop; that ore trains, after the final run to the harbor, toss cinders at their dead eyes; and that, at some time, the whole place gives up and caves in like East Chicago, Gary, and Michigan City. That's how I hate the smoke, soot and people. Then I'll turn off the sign of my heart and throw away the map.

But the hills get bigger. People in the bars know what I do. I wait outside for them to bring me beer. Then we drive to Connor's Point for a drink. Then, depending upon the stars and the moon—

Heartbreak Hotel would be obscured in my mind if it weren't for the sign going on and off. Bob Harris. Bob Harris. The biggest sign on the waterfront reads DANCING. You don't see a building, but the red neon DANCING sign of Johnny's Tavern. Sometimes I go dancing. The Whoop 'n Holler Tavern, on the other hand, has a revolving light on its roof. The light guides the drinkers and drunks, who also guide me from the dance floor. Abigail's Dirty Shame Saloon has other enticements. All Heartbreak has is the jukebox and the sign of a broken-down heart. You hear the music all up and down North 3rd, echoing over the water and off the bows of rusting ships just a broken heartbeat away.)

Stan Harris, the old man, puts himself on automatic pilot every day of the year. It's remarkable to see him go through the fog to the bar—left on Banks, right on Baxter, foggy, two-block jaunts down alleys, right on North 3rd. He comes rolling down North 3rd with the fog and is silent walking. In the gray, curling mist, you can't hear a thing. There will be a tan jacket up ahead and a man inside saying "How are you?" Pierced by this arrow called "the Head of the Lakes," he's no more than an outline in the fog.

"What are you doing?" he asks at three A.M.

"I can't get rid of the spots," she says. She's rubbing her fingers. They've turned red. He sees a fine dust. Her arms and neck have red marks. Some on her neck under the rouge are an inch wide.

"They don't hurt," she says, "but bother me. What do you suppose, Stan? Am I becoming a rose?"

She gets up for a bath. She's been attempting to cover the things on her arms.

"I brought some beer," he tells her. He turns down the pressure cooker. I draw her bath, fix her couch.

"What are these?" he whispers. They look like petals of a corroded rose.

"Do they come off her arms?" I ask.

He tosses them in a wastebasket. "I don't know," he says.

"Did you clean the bathtub, Magda?" he asks when she's done. She doesn't answer. He tries again. "Did that *National Geographic* come for the boy? Do you want a beer?"

"No, no, I'm tending my roses," she says from bed.

"So you're not thirsty. I'll have one myself then. And if you're gonna stay in there, I might as well damn shut off the humidifier."

He brings a beer to her room, setting it on the nightstand. "I guess I'll be off to bed. I cleaned my dishes." He kisses her forehead. We notice the fine powder on the pillowcase around her head.

"You coming to sleep?" he asks me.

"Yeah."

The old man turns on the vaporizer. It sputters and puffs. The windows steam up.

"No," she says as I leave her room.

Before sleep, I dream of roses. All of a sudden they line the side of our house. They are a deep, rich red. Sometimes they nod very slightly in the fog . . .

Up here in Superior, which in the old man's mind stands at the angle in the letter "L" in the words WATER, LIGHT & POWER CO. at the gas plant; in this part of the world, northwest winds bring rain and fog that corrode everything, even the goodness of your heart. Both the lake and the town lie frozen solid the other months of the year. This is what happens during the five frozen months: drinking becomes heavy, the drinkers become desperate, life hangs suspended in the ice, the foghorns blow, hearts tear and break away in the cold. Once in the dark months a man propositioned me with a box of government cheese.

"It's all I've got. No money left, and I heard you were an understanding kid."

"No," I told him, "it's gotta at least be for beer money."

I dream of never going again to Heartbreak Hotel. I dream of saving money and hitting the good bars. I'd go up the street and put my broken heart behind me. I'd dance at the Androy. Fast or slow, it wouldn't matter . . . whatever they wanted, just so some day I danced out of here on the arm of a stranger.

My old man passes the gas plant almost every day going to work. There's this huge metal globe maybe three stories high for the storage of natural gas. Four steel legs hold it up.

"It's like a little world," he always says. "Lookit . . . there's the gas core, the steel sides . . . then we got the bay and air and water. All of it, all the elements of life to make it worth living, everything."

Where the equator would be on a map, say, here's a seam bolted by rivets running around the gas-plant globe. SUPERIOR WATER, LIGHT & POWER CO. is painted in blue on the side. With my Ma's six-pack in the crook of one arm, the old man points with the other. "Lookit, that's the Great Lakes up there where it's painted blue," he says. "Lookit at Detroit and Cleveland. Detroit's right where the bottom of the 'G' starts its turn to go up. See the line of rust there? The only rust on the whole globe is around the Great Lakes."

I think of how some day the legs supporting the globe will rust, the globe collapse, the whole city be gassed. I tell him this.

"Gassed or rusted," he says. He sits on the tracks, opens a beer.

It's the weather which causes unprotected things to fall apart. Moisture gets in the wood. In time the wood rots and crumbles under the touch. Iron oxidizes. At first you can rub the rust off with your hand. But if you wait it takes a wire brush and some hard scrubbing. And some things are impossible.

"It's rust," the doctor says, "honest-to-goodness rust." It's a week later. "Your wife is rusting to death, Mr. Harris. Do you understand?"

She is out of hearing in the next room at the clinic.

"Her blood has excess iron," the doctor says. "You don't normally get hemochromatosis if you aren't taking iron pills, and you've said she wasn't."

"No," Pa says.

"We're gonna have to bleed her each week. Her skin's going to bronze. It'll only get worse. Her body's an old car."

"I believe it's the air," Pa says.

"It could be," says the doctor.

We take her home. She's got gloves. Around her poor, dear red neck she has tied a scarf to keep moisture out. A foggy, wet afternoon, the sun has little chance of breaking through. It's close to three o'clock. We'll fix dinner, fill the vaporizer, put her to bed. No, no vaporizer . . . but we'll make her comfortable in other ways. It'll be best to keep her dry.

The old man is confused. He needs a drink. He's shaking more and more. "What if it's contagious?" he says. "Ain't we seen rust laying waste to Duluth-Superior?"

He's right. It spreads from building to building, over railroad tracks. It eats at ore boats behind Heartbreak Hotel. I think of an Edgar Allan Poe story we read in high school. Now it's like the Red Death has the right-of-way here, too.

Ma ain't happy. She makes coffee and sits at the table as he empties water from the vaporizer. "At least I know how I'll go," she says, "no more wondering."

"I'm drying every bit of water in the tub and sink. I'm wiping down the windows, Ma," I say. Then I turn on her TV shows.

"I'll be going out awhile. I've got a lot to think about, Mag," says the old man who can hardly control the shakes. He's got a woman at the bar. Younger than him, he calls her his "Dolly." This has been going on for ten years.

"I understand why you're going," she says.

"But I don't understand it, Ma. I know you're a rose and shouldn't he stay home? Shouldn't he? I know you're just a beautiful rose. Why does this happen?" I ask her. She's all by herself and vulnerable to atmospheric conditions.

The fog will hit him. He'll feel it seeking places to enter his unfastened cuffs. Hoping to carry less moist air into his lungs, he'll bundle the coat about him and breathe through his nose. It's how he is. There's no money for hospitals or for bleedings, so he'll stumble down the alley to Heartbreak Hotel, which won't make many things better. The old man's got iron in his heart, but it's different from Ma's. He won't rust, his heart'll just get hard. And why is this, I wonder, that some are spared? He'll make jokes. "Call the junkyard," he'll say, "see what price scrap metal's getting!"

A perilous fog has come between us all. I know of no place that isn't rusting. All her married life my mother has sat here watching TV and becoming proficient in the Art of Pressure Cooking. He never took her anywhere. And before that, when she was a working girl, she stayed in too. Now her heart is oxidizing.

He calls, crying over the telephone. "I'm drinking. Lemme talk to Ma." I don't put her on. I know rust is attacking the hearts and homes of out-of-work men—in Detroit, Cleveland, Buffalo, in all the cities and towns where plants have shut down and where the dampness invites its way in. They have nowhere to go but the Whoop 'n Holler, Dew Drop Inn, and Boiler Room Tap.

It's from disuse. The men in Cleveland and Detroit are rusting from disuse. Now my own mother suffers this affliction. The old man for years left her home when he'd go to work. Without purpose in life, she took no precautions against rust, just sat home putting moisture cream on her face, bathing whenever she chose, and using the vaporizer freely. Sometimes she'd leave water standing in dirty dishes. It was that, the hemochromatosis, and the disuse . . .

The next morning we see a used car dealer about rust protection. Not before the old man reads up on oxidation, however. Before he can sweep, mop, and empty ashtrays, the stools are occupied, so I have to help him.

"Bump 'n a beer?" he asks the customer.

Behind the bar, pickled pig's feet nestle in a jar of cloudy water.

"Nah, beer today . . . Little under the weather las' night."

"Big head, Ern?" the old man asks another customer.

"Yeah."

"Bowl or glass, Gus?" All day long it's the same.

"Bowl."

"Joe, what's for you this morning?"

"Maybe some Petri's will warm me up. What d'you think?"

"Here's to ya," the old man replies and rings it up.

That's where the picture is, "Le Tombeau des Lutteurs," hanging behind the cash register. The words, "The Tomb of the Wrestlers," are printed at the bottom. It's copied from a real painting by this French guy of a room in somebody's house. You can't see much of it, just some shadowy blue corners, because of all things, what's growing right inside takes up all the space. What is it but a rose, a big rose whose petals are red, deep, and inviting? It just kind of overwhelms the room and the air in it. But I don't understand the title.

Ma's never taken iron pills, but iron is there. If she cuts herself, she'll bleed it. "'The rusting of iron—'" Pa reads in *Elementary Metallurgy*. He reads so loud and hard the customers look up. "'Iron combines with oxygen and water . . . forms hydrated iron oxide.' What does it all mean?" he asks. He goes on some more. "'The oxide is a solid which retains the same general form as the metal from which it was formed, but is porous and somewhat bulkier. Being soft and weak, it renders iron useless for structural purposes.'"

I start then. "'Fortunately for the peace of mind of the beginning rose grower, the rose is an exceptionally tough and normally healthy plant and is troubled by relatively few diseases or cankers.'" It's from *Roses for Every Garden*. The old man's watching. "'Diseases behave in a rather peculiar manner.' Listen now," I say. "'They may appear during one summer and not another, so the fact that a disease attacked this year does not necessarily mean it will come again to plague you next year.' See! Ain't it proof?" I ask.

But as I discover how to care for roses, he discovers how to prevent rust: iron can be alloyed, which makes it resist corrosion; it can be treated with a substance that would "react preferentially with air and water, and thus, while being consumed, protect the iron," says his book; or it can be covered with "an impermeable surface coating" so that air and water don't reach it. I read him more about roses, "in case of die-back, shoots blacken"; he reads me more about rust.

"Which one you guys want?" he asks the customers.

"Rust," they say.

We keep reading back and forth till noon, then go to the used car dealer after that, then to the hardware, where the old man buys a gallon of Rust Pruf. He applies it to his head, neck, and arms out in the alley. "Here, you too," he says. He tries Four in One Oil, deciding it's too expensive for Magda, whose terrible roses have grown considerably. She's got a whole garden in there. She nurses their stems and petals tenderly. She won't let him near.

I don't believe it's rust, though, and when he goes back to see his Dolly at the bar, I read the directions on a canister of Ferti-Lome Rose Dust. "It says here I've gotta 'hold duster 12–18 inches' from you, Ma." She's sleeping. I don't talk loud. "You're 'the surface to be dusted.' Let's see, 'Apply Ferti-Lome Rose Dust in such a manner that a uniform, hardly visible coating results on both sides of foliage.'" I shake the can, sprinkle it out. Suddenly her rust turns white with powder. Ma's a beautiful, red rose who has only me to keep off the aphids, the dipterous leaf miners, or the two-spotted spiders.

A postcard: Superior, Wisconsin, pop. 28,000, has two, actually three things to set it apart. It has 1) the highest rate of alcoholism per capita for any city of its size in the country; 2) the "World's Largest Freshwater Sandbar," which is a long, sandy beach bordered by the lake on one side and a bay on the other; and 3) the "World's Largest Ore Docks," which are three in number, but only one in actual use. At nine o'clock on the night of the dusting and sprinkling, I get a phone call from someone who wishes to meet me behind the Whoop 'n Holler.

Now the rest of a word postcard: The N.P. Ore Dock, like the globe at the gas plant, stands about a mile from home, but in another direction. From either side of the dock, long metal chutes, which are rusty like everything else, hang over the water. Railroad engineers once positioned locomotives over the chutes. Now there is a different sort of positioning going on below. In the old days, ore slid down the lowered chutes into the open holds of ships. It made a curious sound, an avalanche of ore against steel. On still summer nights you'd hear the sound of commerce in the harbor, a sound I heard the night I "shipped out."

I was working for the old man, waiting on tables and booths until after midnight. I was, you might say, a "deckhand." It was three years ago, I was still in high school, when this old sailor off of the Mantadoc came up. That was a Canadian ship. You can tell by the "doc" of the name, which means Dominion of Canada.

"All ahead two-thirds, Mate?" he said.

I didn't know what he meant, but he left money for me and a note: "Let me trim your jib."

He returned the next night. "All ahead—?"

"You got a car?" I asked. I was frightened of who would know.

"Got plenty of money and a rented car," he said.

"Do I have to sit in the bosun's chair?" I asked.

"We'll see about it, Mate," he said.

"I need money and beer then."

"Steady as she goes, Mate," he said.

He said it again as he eased toward me in the back seat of a rental car under the N.P. Ore Dock. "Steady now . . . steady as she goes. All ahead one-third?"

"All ahead," I repeated.

"Two-thirds then?"

"Two-thirds then."

It was the sound of commerce. I'd hear it again and again after that. It always left me crying, my heart broken. That was the start of my career at sea. Night after night now the ore carriers whistle departure and the tug responds.

Ma wasn't afflicted with aphids that night when I came home sorry. She'd done this type of work herself out of a house at 314 John Avenue. I carried on tradition. I washed up, kissed her, went to sleep dreaming that someday there'd be no use for me . . . that, unprotected, my Heartbreak Hotel sign would fall away in the fog and be replaced by something else, a flower shop sign maybe. To have someone watch out for you in the world, that's what mattered, I kept thinking. I awoke at two when the old man rolled in singing "O, Canada." I didn't want to go it alone into the night, but I had Ma then and so didn't worry. As much as I hated Stan Harris, the old man, I loved Magda Harris, my Mom.

The old man calls her "Hagda" and always has. His books may be correct about her. I don't see it this way. I see her as a rose.

The rust follows the general form of her old, shapeless body. It rises for the mole on her neck and falls for the deep scar on her leg. Her voice has changed. It's become tinny. For two months she's been giving orders.

"Tighten the lid on the pressure cooker," she says. I thought she was talking to me, thought she knew what I'd been doing with my nights.

"Yes, Hagda," the old man says.

"You emptied the vacuum bag lately? How are the dishes? You want an old woman to get up from her rustbed? Not on your life! I'm *glad* it's almost over."

Everything I touch is oily. Sometimes the old man forgets about moisture. He uses the steam iron, puts on the vaporizer, leaves water standing in the tub.

"Check for humidity in here," she says.

He understands the chemical process of corrosion, but he just huffs and argues and does nothing.

In Ma's rust-encased brain, she is shutting him out, turning her corroded back on him. But by doing it she's leaving me out, too. Her legs get red-rose marks.

"Don't do this, Ma. I'm unprotected. I don't have anyone to look after me," I tell her. "I don't want to be up on deck alone in the world. I'm afraid of being a deckhand. Something bad's gonna happen to me."

Then these bronze circles appear on her which begin to fall off.

"Please, Ma, please," I say.

The fine dust we saw on her pillow appears everywhere. Her fingers are growing brittle. They rust and flatten. She can't walk far. "Be careful of road salt," I tell her in early November. When she strikes her hands together they make a sound which infuriates Pa. She's not much to look at. Rusty parts fall off. Her voice sounds sharp and brittle as though it's coming through a tin aperture or horn, as through a steel pipe. " 'tanle', brin' me the 'offee." He can hardly stand it that she won't allow him in her garden. "Why should I?" she says.

"You 'ere no goo' t' me (You were no good to me)," she says.

"Magda, I tried. I got you a nice, warm place here. See how nice. Isn't it something to be proud of? Heck, how long've we been together, Mag?"

" 'ort' yea's."

"Yes, almost a golden anniversary coming up. Hang around a few, Mag! Why d'ya want to go this way? Who'm I gonna bring home beer to?"

" 'ut up, 'tanle'," she says. " 'et me sleep!"

One day late in life the old man becomes a philosopher. In all the bars on Tower and 3rd, he's heard of no others who are afflicted with rust, so he begins to search heaven and earth. "Why do you suppose this all is?" he asks.

In Heartbreak Hotel he sits across a table from a guy who's soaking his thumbs.

"Who are we?" Pa asks. I join them. "No, really. I need answers. Who are we?"

"Two drunks," the man says. His face is red. (Think of a postcard of a puffed and veined nose hanging from a guy's face like a magnificent, intricately patterned hive. His thumbs are discolored from hammer blows. One day he invited customers to hit his thumbs, so long as they bought him a beer.) "Have you heard about Magda Harris who used to work over at . . ."

"Don't you know that's my wife?" Pa says. As the man dries and cradles his thumbs, Pa asks him, "Why do people suffer? Why oxidize Magda and not, not . . . you, for instance?"

"I don't know any of it, but I ain't drunk and I know nobody'd give her a burial in her condition. I saw a chunk of metal on the street, a rusted-up fender."

The thumb-and-hammer man goes with us to the dock. Some, but not us, would go to church to find answers to such problems as why human beings must suffer on earth. The dock is a kind of spiritual place for the city and region. Out of this dock ore used to go to rusting cities like Buffalo and Cleveland. We'd give them the raw goods to start them right.

A cinder path runs beneath the arched ceiling. Standing at one end, your view narrows to where the arches come together at the far end. It's an illusion Pa and I enjoy. When you look up at this ore palace you think of churches in town whose ceilings are also meant to elevate the spirit. They have sacred paintings and lights made to look like stars on the ceiling; the docks have, well—

"Who's drawing all those broken hearts here?" the old man asks. It's like someone who's been coming in a parked car maybe, has been counting, keeping score. There are twenty-three broken hearts in all. Bob Harris. Bob Harris, the sign in town says.

In some places the light falls through. It's a good thing most of the path is in shadows, so the old man can't see where my phone number is written in chalk on the walls. The slip hasn't frozen. Water laps at the sides of the dock.

"If she's gonna act that way, I'll revenge myself on earth," the old man says.

The thumb-and-hammer man says, "You know about your heart and mind, what all they can take. You know that if your heart's made of iron, you need to keep it lubricated right every day. You know . . . Look at my thumbs!"

I hear this conversation drifting over the water. The piece of ore stains my fingers when I pick it up. First, a heart on the wall, then—

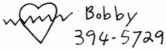

We all walk back to Heartbreak Hotel. On the jukebox Pa plays his favorite tune, "The Swamper's Revenge on the Windfall." "There ain't no rust where there's beer," he says. He drinks six cans of Royal Bohemian. "Oxidize me, boys! Sell me for scrap!" he says. They can't believe his story. He downs a shot of schnapps, a brandy and water, a bowl of beer. "This is my wife," he says. He bangs a tin ashtray on the table, puts one on his head. " 'tanle', brin' me 'ore 'offee 'ow!" He has another glass of beer, then one for the road.

At home Ma is finally, willfully, rusting to death.

"Don't, Ma," I beg.

"G'night, son."

"Ma, fight it . . . don't give in!" It's a deep, rusty sleep she falls into like no one on earth has ever known.

I run to Heartbreak Hotel. "C'mon," I say. I pull at his jacket. As her last, few healthy cells succumb and rust extinguishes the light from her eyes, as her head and heart become totally oxidized, the old man gets a second wind. "C'mon, Pa. C'mon!" He consumes four more beers, a nightcap, and another one for the road. The he decides on an eye-opener. "You son of a bitch," I tell him.

What remains on the couch for us to find at four A.M. is a thin red strip of what used to be my mother. The old man fidgets with his collar, then stares to where Ma's rusted arm is thrown back over her head as though pointing a finger at Pittsburgh. The old man is moved. Taking her in his arms, he hugs her and cries. He scratches himself on her rusty arms. He'll have to be more careful, he says.

The thumb-and-hammer man was right. No one will bury a person whose life has corroded. We leave her on the couch till we can think of what to do. It takes the old man two weeks. "The hardest part will be getting her down there," he says.

Then one late afternoon he hauls the wagon out of the garage. He has been in the bar all day, and struggling with the wagon and with Ma helps to clear his head. "That's a fine girl, Mag. Here we are," he says. Embracing her brittle, blushing body, he realizes how unfair life can be. He stares deep into her rusty eyes. "There now," he says to soothe her.

What secrets could you tell me, Ma? What secrets of the deep, selfish pleasures of oxidation? Where have you gone, where do I look for you?

Pa runs the rope through a hole where her hip has rusted, then ties the rope around the wagon to offer some stability. One day, I think to myself, university archaeologists digging at the base of what looks like a temple or ore palace of some fantastic shape may find what they believe to be evidence of an age long disappeared, an age characterized by men who'd do anything, even smash their fingers, for a sip of beer. Pa looks at his own. All there in fine shape. He wouldn't have to be like the thumb-and-hammer man.

"It wasn't bad enough that he humiliated her," I tell the thumb-and-hammer man some days later, "then he had to *humidify* her."

"What else?"

"Exposed her to road salt!"

"What else?"

"Bathed her too often."

"Yeah? What motive?"

"Beer money," I say.

"Now, kid," he says. "It's Bobby, ain't it? Your Daddy's a fine man, as good a fellow as—"

"But he humidified her!"

"Kid, I'll tell you something I heard about you, Bobby. I heard about the docks. You better watch your tongue. Now you go home and listen well to your Papa . . . as good and kind a one as the day is long."

Pulling the wagon beside the railroad tracks, my old man stops to salvage a rusty bolt laying half-buried in weeds. Another time he pries out a hunk of iron ore fallen from a boxcar and tosses it in the wagon with his beloved. He'd have plenty to remember her by. He'll keep these things in his drawer, I think, maybe even pray to them. Some day when he's real old and living in a room behind Heartbreak Hotel, he'll pull out the rusted bolt and tell some visitor, "This is my good, dear wife who preceded me in death."

Now even the sun sinking through layers of industrial smoke over West Duluth looks old and rusty. "We've had a good life, ain't we, Mag?" the old man asks. "Sure we did. Things all worked out. Don't ya see, Mag, it's a wonderful, beautiful sunset to your life," he mutters to keep from sobbing. He can't cry. He's being careful of moisture.

But I, Bob Harris, can't stop crying. I've got no one now, nothing but Heartbreak Hotel. I am left unprotected to hate his life, his sobbing, his excuses.

*   *   *

You'd be able to tell how deep she went by how long water kept rolling up to the surface. The old man lugs her to the edge. He wears gloves to protect himself from cuts and scratches. I, on the other hand, desire her violent, sharp edges to mark my arms.

He has hauled what passes for Ma all the way from home down the Great Northern tracks, then down the cinder path to the end of the dock—and nobody will do anything about it. ("He vaporized her," I told the thumb-and-hammer man. "He exposed her to relative humidity. He was the relative behind it all.")

Careful not to snag his clothes, the old man gives her one last heave and rolls her in. "I hate to see it happen like this," he says. The water in the slip is deep, for the wake of Ma's passing takes up one whole minute. Then there are bubbles. Pa dusts himself off as he mutters a prayer over the dear departed. To him she's become a rusty old hulk, nothing more. In his coat pocket he rummages for a few remaining petals to scatter over the bay. That done, he mutters something else and strolls back to Heartbreak Hotel where he's left some change on the bar.

It's just me, the wagon, and the fog. As the sun sets, the fog rises with the moon. Night after night, month after month, it billows in. It dampens your face and sometimes obscures the mean edge of life around the warehouses and docks on lower 3rd. On some nights when it's real bad all you'll see on the whole street is a broken heart, or plenty of broken hearts ducking back into the doorsteps as you pass. Aching for love, I stand out among them. Drunks strolling by, sometimes a sailor, I'll whisper, "All ahead two-thirds?"

I've been hurt at it a few times. Unprotected things fall apart in the rain, I've found. A gentleman I met once had no transportation. We took the bus to the end of the line where he rang me off. Another time a sailor on the Richfield went Full Throttle when I'd asked for Reverse. Then Ma died. Then the elderly

Canadian returned to trim me. "Steady . . . steady," he implored. "Give me the steam . . . Full ahead!" he cried, and it was too much for me and I got out of there without my five dollars pay.

I've broken my heart all over town. On every pillar of the docks, I've drawn them in ore dust. On every park bench in Superior, I've carved them with stones and knives:

The River of the
Flowering Banks

I don't remember where we'd found the plastic cards. Now after all these years I've found another one—in a missal in an upstairs drawer.

On one side is a little calendar. "Brown Fish are Days of Total Abstinence," it says. "Red Fish are Days of Partial Abstinence." The days of each month are printed in brown and red ink. Some, like February, don't have numbers but a lot of fish, like this:

	S	M	T	W	T	F	S
Feb.	15	16	17	🐟	19	🐟	🐟

We'd been sitting by the river.

"What's Wednesday, February 18?" he'd asked me. Gerald Bluebird was a Chippewa Indian.

"Red Fish," I said.

"You always get 'em right."

"Give me May 20!"

"Brown Fish," he said.

"Nope," I said.

That was long ago. Sometimes when I walk into the house now, if Pauline and the kids are gone, maybe for a second I feel like I'm back there. Things haven't changed. The house looks the same. I guess these are landmarks—the house, the plastic card with the fish, the way the refinery work whistle blows at one o'clock every day, but I don't have to answer it.

My own father and Mr. Bluebird worked at the Fredericka Mill. The place ran seven days a week. They didn't have time off. Thankfully, I have my own business, which Pauline sees to during the afternoons. Gerald Bluebird and I had no cabin at Balsam Lake or anything like it in the old days. In summer we'd work free for the nuns, stacking books or cutting the school lawn. We were eleven and though we didn't enjoy serving Mass every day then going right over to work for Sister Benitia, now when I think back, we still had time to hang around the river.

Gerald Bluebird's sister got married.

"My social calendar says it's the day before the fifth Sunday after Pentecost. The Friday before it has a brown fish," Gerald said when we found out there'd be a wedding. "That means 'Total Abstinence.'" He was looking in the missal.

"Are you under the right column and year?"

"Page 419 . . . 1958, right?"

"1959!" I said.

I remember he had trouble with history.

We really looked forward to the wedding. Instead of getting up early, putting on the cassock and surplice at church, filling the cruets with water and wine, lighting the candles, then helping Father dress, we could get up later that day and do all those things.

Father Nowak would come in. "Hello"—it sounded like "biyce"—"Hello, biyce, Gerald and Ralph."

My name's not Ralph but Warren Slipkowski. Ralph Slipkowski is my Dad. It didn't matter when Father Nowak called me it. I let him call me "Ralph." Sometimes he'd say "Ral . . . uh . . . Warren," which is my real name.

How could you not like him? I've thought over the years about what makes a person tick. Father back then must have been the age I am right now. He was from Toledo—two states and two Great Lakes away from here—but he got along just fine. The different colored chasubles he wore were beautiful. They were these big cloth vestments. They had crosses on both sides, and when he put them on, they hung like a cape in front and back. When he wore violet it was for humility and penitence. White meant purity and black meant mourning. He wore red for Pentecost.

"Green today," he'd say. You had to hand him this rope cord. There's what is called an alb—a white linen robe—and the cord goes around it at his waist. You have to get behind him and hand it to him to tie in front. Then he wore the chasuble last and over everything.

There was this other chasuble too. I'd seen it hanging in the back of the closet where Lu, the housekeeper, kept Father's extra vestments. Out of all of them, this chasuble was something. The missal said it had the power to replace green, white, and red. It was beautiful gold cloth and worn only on occasions of great solemnity. I always figured Gerald Bluebird was impressed, though I never knew what he thought of the priest's vestments.

We were looking forward to the wedding anyway, mainly for the possibility of a tip, as I recall. Gerald and I were serving partners for the whole summer. We did the 7:30 Mass every day. Gerald made sure he filled up the cruets with the water and the wine while I lit the altar candles. I think he did this so he could sample the altar wine. We'd take turns holding the paten for Communion. Some people forgot to put their teeth in before receiving. Or we'd hold the paten under a parishioner's chin, Father would be taking the Host from the ciborium, and the parishioner would sneeze or something right at the last moment. There It went. Was I to pick It up? Gerald? Father Nowak?

When we used to walk out on the altar with the organ playing and the choir singing, Father would say, "*Introibo ad altare Dei,*" then "*Ad Deum, qui laetificat juventutem meam.*" That part always moved me. It meant, "I will go unto the Altar of God. Unto God, Who giveth joy to my youth."

Trudy Bluebird's wedding came a month before the ferryboat and Mrs. Ada Armbuster's funeral. As the nuns got the ants off the peonies, people came in from the reservation eighty miles away for the wedding. Because the Bluebirds were the only town Indians it was an invasion. There were white people at the wedding though, too, for she was marrying Richard Bozinski. *Oh, Trudy, you were beautiful. Your eyes shined with tears under the veil.*

I remember she smiled as Mr. Bluebird gave her away. Father Nowak read the service, then he blessed the rings, which Richard and Trudy exchanged. Then Gerald and I shook hands and the organ played "The Wedding March" and Father shook with us and Trudy hugged Gerald and Mrs. Bozinski hugged me and Father Nowak shook hands with Mr. Bluebird. The Polish people were hugging the Indians from Bad

River and Lac du Flambeau. I'd never seen anything like it. Old people spoke different languages, and everybody lit cigarettes and Gerald and I awaited our tip. We straightened Richard's tie and shined his shoes with our hankies. "That's enough, Gerald," said Mrs. Bluebird. "Don't make fools of yourselves for a buck." Trudy saw it differently and kissed us both. Then Gerald and I sneaked off for a cigarette.

The tip came from Pauline Bozinski, who'd been the nun's best student the year before and whom I couldn't stand then but came to marry fifteen years later in the same church.

"Lot you did to earn this, Warren," she said to me. Instead of handing it to us, she threw the card on the kneeler. "It's from my brother. You wouldn't get a red cent, not an Injin nickel if I was getting married."

"Why, Pauline," Gerald said, laughing.

She left in a huff. At the Polish Club everybody was eating and drinking. The "Polka Dots" played. They were popular then. At the bar some old guy asked me why I wasn't dancing. His face was red from drinking beer and whiskey, and he yelled at me, "Polka or get out!" So I did, walking all the way home. But not before the music stopped and Trudy's cousin Jay held up his hands, raised his drink, and said, "Ladies and Gentlemen, I give you Trudy Bluebird!"

That was the highlight of our summer. The tip came to five dollars. We spent it in two mornings at the Arrow Cafe. I see that Mr. Isaacson, who ran it in those days, died a few weeks ago in his eighties.

There wasn't much to do from then on except wait for Gerald in the afternoons.

It was the month of the Strawberry Moon. The Chippewas around Lake Superior marked summer and fall by the changes in vegetation. Their Flower Moon was in May. Their Strawberry Moon was in June. The Raspberry Moon in July, and so on through the Blueberry Moon, Wild Rice Moon, and Falling Leaf Moon of October.

It was almost the Raspberry Moon by the time the newly-weds took off. The long-fruited thimbleweed was out, the false rue anemone gone for the year. By the time the tall cinquefoil rose to our knees, Gerald and I wondered about the gold chasuble again. Before Father'd come in the sacristy, and when Lu, the housekeeper, wasn't around, we'd rub our hands on it. Gerald promised never to sample the altar wine again.

"How come you don't ever wear it, Father?" I asked one day. Gerald was on the altar extinguishing candles.

"War-ren, it's shust for solemn occay-shuns," he said. "Like when the Bishop comes. Here, biyce," he said. Gerald was back from the altar when Father gave us the ten dollars for serving all summer. After the Arrow Cafe we headed to the river where it was beautiful and quiet and where the pine trees grew and the popple and chokecherry, the star grass and fireweed. After a rain the hill's beautiful, wild looking. Along one side, curving around the cemetery, comes the river. I was there with Pauline and the children where the city wants to put in an access road to the river. The city will wreck everything, all the wildflowers, if they drive down in there.

In the middle of the Raspberry Moon back then something happened. We finally got a funeral, Mrs. Armbuster's. Before that, a few days before it, Gerald had a vision too.

"Jesus!" I was in the popple woods and heard him. "Jesus, Warren, look out on the river!"

It was a ferryboat or something playing music. Downriver half a mile, here it came out of the river fog. It was pink from top to bottom. The gunwales rose a foot or two out of the water, I recall. The river wasn't deep enough for much more than a motorboat in there.

"Lookit!" Gerald Bluebird shouted. And here it was coming, playing some kind of music over the swamp.

We were excited. We ran down to the tamaracks. I remember how the red-winged blackbirds were flying up all over the place.

She had white poles fore and aft, which held up a pink canopy. The canopy kept the deck shaded. Four or five men watched us as she swung close. They were resting on these boxes.

I remember that the river falls off deep there.

"Grab this here," the men yelled to us. "We'll throw it. Wind it around that there." They pointed to a stump. We heard the tinkling music. They pushed some planks over onto the bank, asking Gerald if he'd mind stepping into the river to prop them up with these wood supports. When he got them in, the men came ashore. They started to lift boxes. The guy who steered got them working. "Hey, you kids want to help?" he asked.

"What's in them?" we said.

"Indians," the Captain said.

Two men started uphill. They cursed when the box fell open. We could see a little dust come out.

"Remains of Indians . . . 'Injins,' I should say."

Two more men carried smaller boxes. They bounced over across the planks to shore. The men who steered looked around. "Nice place. You ain't partly Indians yourselves, are you?" he asked.

I was smiling.

Gerald's mouth froze wide open. "No . . . yeah," he said real fast.

They came for more boxes. It looked like they would take all week to unload.

"You get the others back aft, too," the Captain said to them. He turned to us. "These were all buried on the Point. It was a shame disturbing their remains." He knocked on a box. "Anybody home?"

Gerald's face froze from smiling.

"Hey, boys, we're moving these people from out on the Point on the lake. The State of Wisconsin says we have to locate them somewhere else so this company can build on the land. I guess the Chippewas thought the place out there was holy or something. They didn't have markers on the graves."

We walked uphill with him. Gerald Bluebird was very quiet.

"Now, I don't feel good about it," the Captain said, "but what t'hell, they hired us to crate 'em and move 'em. We don't have much of a draft so we can get up where the others can't."

At the top of the hill where the cemetery stands, some boxes were piled.

"They ain't goin' in here. They ain't Cath'lic," one mover yelled. "Put 'em down right at the edge of the hill!" He wore torn clothes, was sweating under the arms. He took a mouthful of Copenhagen, put his boot up on one of the boxes.

Down below, the movers were still coming. They made a path up through the grass. There were shovels now, too.

"My boat's used on Bark Bay to ferry the summer tourists. It's a party boat."

"We gotta get going," said Gerald.

"Come back later," the Captain said.

That happened on the eighteenth day of the Raspberry Moon. On the twenty-first day they buried Mrs. Armbuster in the ground. All the while, the ferryboatmen dug up the hill with no regard for its flowers.

Gerald and I were now happy we had the Church. We'd seen a lot. We'd gone to the river one day, and they'd made us look into a box when the captain was gone. There were splinters and chips and dust in there. A guy handed us a plastic bag.

"I will go unto the Altar of God . . . Unto God, Who giveth joy to my youth."

It was sad. Gerald saw something even worse. He couldn't unfreeze his face. He didn't talk at all before we started Mrs. Armbuster's funeral. We helped Father into the black chasuble. During the Requiem Gerald mumbled the responses. I spoke loud to cover up for him. When Father Nowak stepped to the casket, Gerald just stood up on the altar swinging the censer.

The missal read:

The priest receives the sprinkler from the assistant (that was me) and, having made a low bow to the crucifix, goes round the Bier, and sprinkles the Corpse thrice on each side; then, returning to his place, he receives the censer from the assistant (that was Gerald Bluebird) and in like manner goes round the Bier, and incenses the Corpse in the same way as he sprinkled it; then, having returned the censer to the assistant, he says:

V. And lead us not into temptation.
R. But deliver us from evil.
V. From the gate of hell.
R. Deliver her soul, O Lord.
V. May she rest in peace.
R. Amen.

"Eternal rest grant unto her, O Lord: and let perpetual light shine upon her," Father said.

"Lord have mercy," people cried over Ada Armbuster. "Christ have mercy."

The river was pretty where we buried her. We'd had a little rain the night before, a south wind came up, and the air was heavy with the smell of aspen. You could see the river come curving around below and the tied-up ferryboat with boxes. The pallbearers finally commended Ada to the grave. Father Nowak stooped down to incense her again, because she was pretty deep in. Then they tossed dirt on top of her and were done.

"Let's go. I wanna get back and out of this stuff," I said.

Gerald didn't say anything. Handing over the censer, he took off his cassock and surplice and headed for the Indian graves. He sat a ways off, watching the movers. When the Captain waved, Gerald waved back. One of the men called Gerald an "Injin." "There's one," he said. "Don't let him get away."

Father Nowak and I were in the funeral car. "Warren," Father said. "Where is he?"

"He doesn't feel good," I said. "He'll walk it. We've been watching them move boxes." I told Father what we'd seen.

He answered me differently than I thought he would. He said how Gerald Bluebird must've wanted to be alone to feel bad. Father had a way of looking at you. He'd known the things a young man suffers for and that it wasn't necessarily bad if you wanted to feel that way. Mr. Lenroot was driving. Father Nowak was in front. You never knew what Father would do.

"War-ren," I remember he said, "Indian people, they—"

"Speaking of Indians, catch the scores, Father?" Mr. Lenroot asked like he wasn't listening.

"No," Father said.

"They beat Bob Turley last night in New York."

"Warren," Father said, which really surprised me. "Look at 'er this way . . . you've got to look at things differently than how Sister Benitia at school or how the nuns teach you to look at the world," he said. "We didn't none of us discover America, not me, not the Sisters. Not me and you especially, Warren, we're Polish."

"I know," I said.

I saw him in the sacristy later. He was looking through some chasubles.

When I got back out to the cemetery, I told Gerald Bluebird that we didn't get a tip and that I could have brought him some cake from the get-together after the funeral if he'd said something.

He was glum. The pink ferryboat rode empty.

"You never made nothing before about being Indian. Heck, I thought we were pretty much alike," I said. "Why all of a sudden now?"

His face had the same look it had since something hit him about our church, about the vestments the priest wore and the way they sprinkled and incensed you if you were Catholic.

"What they ever do for us?" he asked.

"Who?"

When the sun caught him, his hair was so black it shined. I'd never seen it like that on Gerald Bluebird. He had these quiet, brown eyes and high cheekbones, and he never started trouble. Nobody ever paid him much attention. Only a couple times did he take the Indians' side in anything, like when we walked home from the 1950s version of the movie *The Last of the Mohicans,* which must've touched something inside of him, because he called me "white man."

I was a little above him on the hill. It was like that moment wasn't fair for Gerald Bluebird because he was the Indian kid who served Mass at St. Adalbert's and he figured that made him the white man's Indian, but then he saw how the church treated people—Catholic or not. "Lookit how they dug 'em up out there on the Point and just threw them down anywhere! Where's the service? Where's anything . . . did anybody notice that?"

I can remember thinking I didn't want Gerald Bluebird to go away. Looking back on it now, I sensed that maybe we were getting older and would go to different schools and grow up with different friends and maybe someday move away from here. I didn't want it to happen, I remember, because in town you knew when it was one o'clock by the refinery whistle and you knew where and who you were—unless you were Gerald Bluebird. I sure thought I knew who I was before all this happened. I knew I'd hated Pauline Bozinski back then and I knew Gerald and I would always be good friends. Then this thing had happened, and suddenly I wasn't sure about anything.

"What'd Catholics do but convert us Indians?" he said. He kind of looked around. He was trying to be strong. But in the star grass and fireweed, and with the ferryboat near, he couldn't help it and even lighting a cigarette he couldn't stop what was happening. His eyes filled with tears. It didn't work when he tried talking to me.

"It's hard to figure," I said.

"I'm scared," he finally said.

"Of who?"

"The people. They shouldn't be treated like that. The people in the boxes."

He stared at me, his face dark from the Raspberry Moon. He was handsome, Gerald Bluebird, even with tears in his eyes, and I could see some day he might be a very noble and proud man. *Where are you now? I wonder.*

He finished a Lucky. "This here's sacred," he told me.

We lay back in the grass which sheltered us.

"It's like there are things out there that must've gotten loose from the boxes."

"I don't know," I said.

"They saw it when we buried Mrs. Armbuster. Everybody's paying attention to Mrs. Armbuster and nobody to the boxes."

Up in the sky, these white clouds were rolling past. Some looked like mountains, one really big one like a castle. When the sun went under, the air felt good, and it smelled good in the grass and flowers and I was very content.

"Nobody noticed," he said. "Hard to forgive."

"Not everybody didn't. Father Nowak, what about him?"

"Maybe he did, maybe he didn't," Gerald said.

Thus, we spent the late morning of Mrs. Armbuster's funeral on the twenty-first day of July, 1959.

"What year is it, Gerald?" (He wasn't very good at history.)

"1858."

"1758," I said.

"1658."

We talked a little longer. A grasshopper walked up my arm and sat there a while. "Brown Fish and Red Fish," I said. Gerald smiled.

We smoked half a pack. Gerald had another rolled up in his sleeve.

"What time is it?" I said after a couple more cigarettes.

"What?"

"What time is it? You know, the sun's so high."

Something was catching the light. It was like a great bird or a horse the Indians believed in. It was so bright I could see the second vision of our summer right up behind me. I was blinded and couldn't make it out. "Look, Gerald!" I said.

Real fast he rolled onto his stomach. We'd never seen the gold one worn, or how it could draw in the sunlight and make you shiver. It was for special occasions, the gold chasuble, but there on the hill above the river it came shining out in all directions and moving toward us. Father, I thought, Father Nowak!

I never in my life figured a person could be that smart. Father Nowak shined in the sun. Gerald's hair shined, too.

"This is a solemn day, biyce," Father started saying when he got to us. "The souls of the just are in God's hands." When he began praying it was like he was saying it to the sky. "The torments of wickedness shall not touch them." He kept on as the three of us walked up. "May the Angels lead thee into Paradise," he was saying. "At their coming may the Martyrs . . ."

He sprinkled holy water on the trees, grass, and dirt path nearby. Incensing the graves of the Indians, he prayed in Latin and sang.

It's called "The Asperges" when they sprinkle holy water on Sunday before High Mass. It's a very formal, holy ceremony. He was doing it now. All we needed were candles and a choir. "May the Choir of Angels receive thee," he was saying. Then I incensed him, and he incensed me. He gave Gerald the censer, and we loaded it with incense, and the cemetery was really smoky. But Father Nowak wasn't done yet until he blessed the purple clover, the dandelions, the stones, and the clay. "We're your guests," he said to the graves. Then he said, "It's not much," as we scattered handfuls of the rice he'd brought in a bag. Gerald stripped three cigarettes and threw the tobacco in the wind. We had bread for the graves, too.

Then Gerald gave Father Nowak a Lucky. Father didn't smoke, but that day he lit one, and we sat a while and talked as the smoke rose up through the aspen leaves. Father talked in Polish for a while, and the sexton and some cemetery workers came by to watch and listen. They figured something was happening. The air was so full of smoke and the ground so different they didn't say much. It was like everything was caught and held in that one moment and nothing could move.

An Essay on Language

THIS time in my class were a Hmong, who'd been here five years; a student from Hong Kong, who for some reason wished to be called "Andy"; three from Japan, Mr. Ishida, Mr. Takahashi, and Miss Reiko Tanigawa; and a Vietnamese, who one day caused me great trouble. Actually she caused two disturbances that I recall.

The first, the less serious, was when she read aloud. The other students looked up, for I was speaking to the class and to Mr. Ishida about subject-verb agreement, when she started reading from the workbook. Maybe it was the tale of the bull and the lion. The straight black hair hung about her face so that we couldn't see her looking at the words. But we could hear her soft, patient voice. She was so busy she didn't pay attention to me.

"Miss Nguyen, please!" I said.

"Teacher?"

It was customary in Vietnam to call the instructor "Teacher." I knew this. I'd been there in 1965. We'd stopped in Japan and Hong Kong, too, which was useful to me now in 1992. Then I thought I could pronounce "Nguyen" properly. I remember saying Nguyen Cao Ky when he was premier and I was in DaNang with the 5th Engineers' and Battalion Band.

Now when I pronounced it "Nooyen," she said "Nyen," so we agreed I should stop trying.

"Thanh," she said. I didn't understand what she rattled off after that.

"Speak slower," I said. "Say slowly what you wish to say."

"You should call me Thanh," she said very slowly.

So that was the reading incident near the start of the school year in September. The second disturbance occurred later as their English improved, however slightly. Miss Nguyen was doing well enough. We'd been through subject-verb agreement, transitions between sentences, and pronoun reference errors, and we'd written thesis sentences, paragraphs, even short essays from which I'd found out that "Andy" feared the Chinese coming to Hong Kong in 1997, that Chong Vang, my Hmong, who wore a strand of yarn about his wrist, had once narrowly escaped the Viet Cong, and that Masanori Ishida deplored the easy life of American university students vs. their Japanese counterparts. In a paper written in pencil, Miss Nguyen told me she'd hoped to go to a medical college, but failed the first "concourse" exam and ended up working two years as a secretary in Saigon City Hall.

"You must explain to me *concourse*," I said. "I don't understand. What do you mean by *concourse?*" I looked out the window. There was construction work all over campus.

"French word, Teacher. I *doan* know," she said. She smiled. She wore colorful dresses, with dark greens and bright yellows like the jungle. Her hair was black. The frames of her glasses were black. Half the time I didn't understand her.

The Japanese were easier to decipher. I smiled back. It is easier to smile than to listen sometimes. When you are forty-six and going nowhere, why do you have to do anything at all you don't want to? Why listen? The war was over. We'd lost. Why was she taking English 100? The war was over.

They brought them in by helicopter. I was nineteen. Wearing a helmet with a white cross taped on the top, I'd run out to the landing place and stand straight up with my arms in a "Y." Miss Thanh is thirty-nine. She's going places I am not. *Sometimes they'd kick them out the helicopter's door. Not even waving to me, the helicopter pilot and his machine gunner would just take off into the sky. Blindfolded, the men were dressed in black pants. Hands tied behind their backs, they were ready for bed. I would lead them in a line to the motor pool . . . to sit them down . . . to rest them. I would force them onto their stomachs. Sometimes we'd kick them.*

"Teacher!" Miss Nguyen said. I hadn't looked at her paper. I wasn't paying attention to their papers. They were writing them in class. The topic I gave them was, "What Was the Nicest Thing Anybody Ever Did For You?"

"Yes, this is good," I said. I leaned over her desk. She'd written four paragraphs. I have the paper. *I kicked the one. Usually they did what you said. They were scared, maybe even innocent peasants, not VC at all. This one was scowling. He started talking back in gook, his head going all over the place. I put a rag in his mouth . . .* Her paper read:

I was born, grew up in a big family. So my mother and my oldest sister had worked very hard everyday to take care all of us. The seven children lived in the same house until the one who found a job and left and so on for the rest.

The thing that I have never forgotten that my mother is the best mother of ours. She helped, cared, and comforted when we needed her. I remember the evenings after school, we ran through miles of rice field and got home with starving stomach, the hot meals were there for us. My mother had saved from pennies to nickels just for the children's food and school. She encouraged us to study every day and night. She told us that she would like to see us to become good persons in community.

And one thing more I haven't forgotten was how the last minutes my brother and I would say to my mother for leaving the native country. He came in out of the jungle. She walked along with us to the local bus station. As I got on the bus, my brother look around. She still stood on the road with her tears. She waited to wave her hand to say good bye forever. I left on bus. My brother—

"Miss Nguyen. This is good," I said. "But look here in line three . . . you need an 'of.' Can you see? . . . *that I kicked as he was falling . . . in the ear . . . as he fell, I . . . in the same ear I am talking to you in . . . your brother that you know I kicked* . . . Miss Nguyen?"

"Teacher?"

"It's this line about your mother. It's too confusing. Also look at this other sentence. 'The thing that I have never forgotten that my mother is the best mother of ours.' Let's change the thing, *change the country.* Don't think Vietnamese. Think English or don't think . . ."

I wasn't looking at her ear or her face. I began to write with her pencil. She was hidden behind her black hair and her black eyes, the jungle. *I knew VC were crawling along the perimeter.* Thanh Nguyen must've been young, hidden in the jungle, I thought. "Let's write it this way. 'I have never forgotten the beauty and kindness of my mother.' Don't you see it's clearer?" I went through some more sentences, adding an ending or a word. It must have been very hard for her to leave Vietnam, I thought. She was not so bad. She was smiling, Thanh Nguyen.

I could feel her beside me. Miss Tanigawa and Mr. Ishida were looking. "I'll just add this 's'," I said. I only thought Miss Nguyen had a cold from the autumn weather. But they were all looking at us—from Japan, from Laos and Hong Kong, which in five years was to revert to China. They'd left their desks and their papers. She was hiding it. I could feel her sobs as she crossed her arms and hid behind her hair so I wouldn't see. It didn't matter that the others saw. "*Ma mére, ma mére,*" she was whispering.

"Miss Nguyen, do you miss her? Is that why? Is it how I've changed your essay?"

I was forty-six, I thought, and going nowhere . . . a Westerner. I didn't need to listen. I gave her the pencil. I could have told her about my mother, who was gone now. I used to write my mother from Vietnam. She died while I was there.

I went to the blackboard. Thanh Nguyen hid in her hair in the jungle. I couldn't see her ear. *This one had talked back to me. It was an incident of war.* I stared out at the campus and the ugly city on Lake Superior. Some guys at the Vets Center called them gooks. *It was an incident of war with the rag and all.* Twenty-seven years later, they were still calling them gooks.

"*Mam,*" Mr. Vang said very softly.

"Write it down," I said.

"Our word for *mother*," he said. He wrote it on the board.

"*Ma ma*," said Mr. Chi-Hanh Tse. He spoke it in Chinese.

"*Okâsan*," said the two Japanese, Mr. Ishida and Mr. Taka-hashi.

"Mother?" I said. "Is that what it means?"

"Write it down," they said.

I put it on the board.

"How you say it in colloquial *Englash?*" Miss Tanigawa said.

"Mom or Ma," I said.

"Can you write it for us?"

I put it up.

"Don't erase the board when I leave," I said. "Leave it up for a while." I looked out the window again. *The Red Cross delivered the message by the same copter I signaled down with a white cross on my helmet and with my arms in a big "Y." My news came with the prisoners. "Here!" the machine gunner had yelled as he pushed out six VC. They started running, blindfolds and all. The helicopter blades blew their hair about. "Here!" He was handing it to me, a telegram from my sister. "Thanks," I said. I stepped back, gave the pilot the signal to take off. Some other guys rounded the gooks up. It was mail for me. I was happy, an unexpected mail call: "Ma died . . . Funeral Sat.," it said. "Can you come?"*

Twenty-seven years ago I read it. I was in South Vietnam thinking of Ma. She'd died. I hadn't been there. Now someone else was thinking of home. Now someone was replacing me. *I didn't mean it, I thought . . . none of it, none of it about her, your mother. I didn't mean changing your words.* "Leave it," I said. "Leave the lines in your papers as they are and go home. All of you. They're pretty good sentences . . . pretty good papers. All of yours are."

Never able to pronounce it right, they said, "Thank you, Mr. Vanka-wicz." They walked out very slowly, Miss Nguyen going back into the jungle.

Outside, some university workers were ripping up the sidewalks. There was always work going on. I watched them from the window. It was getting late. I wrote on the board, PLEASE SAVE. I was saving it. I'd wait all night to keep the janitors away from it if I had to. I'd make sure of it. This is how Mr. Ishida had written the word: お⁻ケだこ又 *Okâsan,* Mother.

Ma mére, I thought and looked away. I sat there a long time. It was already dark when I started copying their words on the blackboard, drawing them the way they'd done it. In Japanese and Vietnamese, in Chinese and Hmong, there are many words for mother. I kept writing them on the board. Then the night school students came in.